Vermyear Academy

A Marcayla K

Vermyear Academy
Copyright © 2017 by A Marcayla K

Library of Congress Control Number:	2017946255
ISBN-13: Paperback:	978-1-64045-643-3
PDF:	978-1-64045-644-0
ePub:	978-1-64045-645-7
Kindle:	978-1-64045-646-4

Printed in the United States of America

LitFire
PUBLISHING

LitFire LLC
1-800-511-9787
www.litfirepublishing.com
order@litfirepublishing.com

Contents

Acknowledgement

I'd like to thank my close friends and family for inspiring me to create this story. In addition, I'd like to give gratitude to my mother and especially my sister. I also want to acknowledge my appreciation to Gabe Chavez and Betty Boston for their hard work and efforts to make my dream possible.

Please note that the songs mentioned in this novel do not belong to me and I strictly give credit to the artists and or artist who produced them.

Four walls and a ceiling, like any other place, it's a prison.

****

One touch. That's all it took for me to realize who He, was. One glance. Instant, burning attraction. One statement. "Is that too tight", he whispered in my ear. That's all Sophie wrote down in her notebook. Her hair, dripping wet with rain, handwriting in scribbles, Sophie tried writing something else. Her hand was shaky, trembling, she couldn't determine whether it was because of how angry she was, or how cold she was. Sophie searched desperately around her dark, cold, bedroom. She felt alone, lost and hopeless. She knew that no one, except Him, could free her from this remote trance. Her walls were covered with shadows from the trees blowing in the heavy wind. She was suffocating; the room was closing in and ruin inevitable. Mortification was the only freedom that she found fitting, pulling her toward the edge. Pathetic. Sophie could only blame herself. She was confused, but there's really nothing to be confused about. Inside, her mind, jumble of useless, heavy emotions and wounding thoughts, all of which were negative. Sophie punched her pillow and buried her face deep into its feathery abyss. She willingly transferred all her emotions and thoughts to her lifeless pillow. It was a welcoming, soft escape that soothed her deaden soul. Sophie's numb; heart and all. Her clothes were wet and heavy, flooded with tears and rain, and her skin pale and lifeless. She was shaking uncontrollably. She knew the rain would dry, but would her tears? At that moment, she didn't care, she couldn't feel, she just wanted to be alone with her misery. She wanted to spew out all of her frustration, her anger and her confusion. *I just walked away. I can't believe I just left him there.* Sophie screamed into her pillow as the tears started streaming down her pallid face yet again. Through a teardrop, her glance caught the crumpled, mucky, white canvas drawing lying beside her bed. It had been transformed into an abstract drawing of smudged pencil markings from the unforgiving rain. The torrent had made its own masterpiece of smeared nothingness that she didn't care to embrace. Her work tainted, she hastily tore the sordid abomination from its dwelling in her sketchbook and crumbled it with both hands before heaving it across the sullen room. She looked down at her hands still shaking and drenched with the sadness of her tears. She was unsure of what to do. The repugnant wad had found its way securely under her computer desk. *Sanctuary*, she thought, "even the rain's masterpiece of nothing could find safety in the shadows". She looked out the window at the unrelenting down pour. The shrill sounds of raindrops taunted her as they hit her bedroom window one after the other, begging the window pane to allow entrance into her perdition. The lightening flashed and the sky exploded into daylight giving the rain false hopes of triumph. The deafening crash of the thunder reprimanded the raindrops and she saw them roll down her window in defeat. Sophie found a little comfort in knowing that the storm was as angry as she was or maybe it's just making a plea, desperate for attention.

9 Months Earlier

'Where Do I Begin?'
The Chemical Brothers

Sophie woke up fuming. She thought to herself, *why would my mom leave my blinds wide open for the sun to grace me with its presence? Brenda knows that I like to sleep in.* She glanced at her clock. "Ok it's 7:30a.m. I can sleep till noon at least."

"SOPHIE!" Brenda yelled from the kitchen, "Your bus comes in-."

"BRENDA, just shut up please I wanna sleep. Is that too much to ask for? Geeze!" Sophie violently turned over in the mess of sheets on her bed and slammed her pillow down, burying her face deep inside it. Her mother walked into the room uninvited. She notices Sophie still lying in her bed still and lifeless. Brenda glides her way through water bottles, coke cans, pieces of paper, and makeup strewn across the floor. She felt like she was trying to glide through quick sand and at any given moment would be embedded in the hoard. She let out a sigh of relief when she finally reached the window. Brenda opened the blinds even wider causing Sophie's eyes to bolt open.

"What the h..."

"I said get up." Sophie gave her mother a Frenchman's wave and turned another 40 degrees in her bed facing the wall. *'Man I wish I could just curse her out right now.'* Sophie's thoughts ran by in her head.

"Well it's the first day of school so uh," Brenda looks at her watch on her wrist. "Oh god, its 7:35 and the bus gets here at like what? 7:45.

And I haven't even had my morning coffee yet. So I suggest you get your lazy behind out of bed and get ready or you'll miss the bus and I'm not driving you to school." Sophie rolled her eyes as a response *Blah blah blah is all I here coming out that loud mouth of hers.* Brenda made her way out of the room the same way she had entered. When she was out of sight Sophie quickly sat up. *I'm glad she can't hear my thoughts out loud because I can just curse her out all day long if I want to. I don't know why she is being so damn annoying this morning. She probably didn't take her Midol. I should have asked her.* Sophie yawned covering her mouth. She could care less if she was late to school; if the school bus pulled off without her then that's the school buses fault for not waiting, not hers.

Sophie just wanted to stay in her cozy little bed and sleep in. She quickly got dressed and didn't say anything to, Brenda, who was making breakfast, and Sophie strutted through the door trying to show off her new flashy shoes to the kids walking to the bus stop while slamming the door behind her. The bus stop was just a block away from her house and saw a few kids already waiting, some of which Sophie didn't recognize and she figured they must have been new to the neighborhood. She placed her backpack in between her feet. Her ex-bestie, Cassandra Reese, gave her a foul gaze. Sophie pretended not to notice, she was sick and tired of Cassandra's nasty attitude.

Sophie forgot about Cassandra after a while, since her new friend Angela started a nasty rumor about Cassandra saying she slept with the whole football team, and Angela blamed it on Sophie. And the thing that surprised her the most was that Cassandra actually believed her which made Sophie livid.

She saw her bus approaching the crowd of eager students waiting on the curb. Immediately Sophie grabbed her backpack and swung it over her shoulder. Sophie was about to get on when who should she see run in front of her and push her out of the way but Cassandra knocking her to the ground. *Why that bitch.* Her fall made a loud thud. A few people snicker and smile as they get on the bus. But her being on the ground didn't matter because the bus still sucked her in against her will. She was pretty certain that the bus driver saw her fall too or probably even heard her, because when she got on, the driver had a smirk on his face.

"What? You're a bus driver, drive." Sophie said carelessly rolling her eyes. The driver just pulled off, tires screeching on the road, not even waiting for Sophie to sit down. She was forced into the first seat and the bus made a couple stops along the way. Some little nerdy kid gets on the bus with no backpack and carrying everything he seemed to need in his arms. He pushed Sophie over and sat down like he was invited.

"Fuck you" Sophie says in a monotone voice.

The boy took out a mayonnaise jar of homemade bubbles.

Is this an omen of what's to come? I sure as hell hope not. The bus made a sudden stop in front of a huge building with what seemed like thousands and thousands of people filing inside. Sophie's stomach churned looking at the massive place. Engraved on the building were the words, Vermyear Academy High School in big black lettering. The building had four walls and a ceiling like any other school, but like any other school to Sophie, it was prison, a prison with a 15 grand a year price tag. As people trailed off the bus, she just sat there, still mesmerized by the building. She never expected to feel so out of her comfort zone on her first day of school. Students whisked, and rushed passed her, rushing off of the bus. *Why are they so excited about going to school? They act like they want to be here.* The rush of students left a lingering smell of cheap cologne and perfume. She found the smell of cologne insufferable.

"Are ya gonna get off young lady? I think school is gonna start soon you better get movin'." The bus driver said urgently. Sophie snapped out of her state of wonder and grabbed her backpack and rushed off the bus. She was looking for her best friend, Ginger, but she was no where in sight. She figured that since it was a new building, she didn't have time to look for her; Sophie noticed that a couple people were looking down at sheets of paper rushing inside. She realized that it was their schedules. *Oh shit.* Sophie thought digging around in her pants pockets for a lump of paper of some kind to calm her nerves down a notch. She rapidly took her backpack from off of her shoulder and practically dumped everything from inside out onto the concrete. All Sophie saw were books, pencils, binders, and folders. *I can't believe*

I already forgot my schedule, and it's the first day.

"Well that's just perfect; this is just the highlight of my day." Sophie mumbled cramming her belongings back in her book bag. *That's okay, you know what, I'm just gonna make up my schedule for the day. Forget my schedule I'll just get it tomorrow.* Sophie strutted through the doors of the school. And this fresh smell of soap and water came to meet her. Air blew past her and through her long hair. The lobby was quiet and had dim lighting. She didn't like when it was silent. It always made her think someone was setting her up and at any moment they'd jump out of the shadows and scare her with a candid camera. She walked passed a room of what looked like the cafeteria. Sophie stopped dead in her tracks to get a good look at it. She never expected it to be so gigantic, she noticed a grand piano right near the entrance with open bay red satin curtained windows. And every table had nice white cloth covering it. *Damn, are they gonna fit everyone and everything in that room at once?* Sophie continued her self guide tour of the school walking and looking at everything with virgin eyes. She walked passed the library and saw three people standing there with violins playing classical music and a person in the far back uncovering a harp. The carpet looked freshly blue, neat, and shampooed and looked like no one set foot in there. *Man talk about paradise.* She was walking on diamonds, the floor was sparkling clean and she could see her reflection everywhere she walked.

'Hmm…lets see what class do I feel like going to?' She looked around for classes that might be near her. Sophie saw the gym filled with mindless sheep running laps. *Damn and it's the first day? Definitely not going in there…maybe I feel like going to biology. If only I can find a room that teaches it.* Sophie made her way up to the second floor. She discovered an isolated room at the end of the corridor. *I guess this one looks promising.* Sophie peeked inside through the glass on the door. *'I'm gonna walk in there like a bad ass cuz I don't give a care.'* Sophie opened the door and it made a loud screech, and everyone in the class had eyes on her, even the teacher. And it was just like silent night. Sophie heard the tune in her head while she was standing there in front of the class room like an idiot. The air stiffened with each second that passed by of the awkward silence. *Oh shit, what do I say? I* didn't even think about that before I walked in. Fuck…um…think Sophie think, think, think. What do I say what do I say?? Sophie's palms became sweaty with every beat her little heart took. *Yeah so much for walking in like a bad ass. I walked in more like a dumb ass.*

"Um…uh…" Sophie stuttered with her words. '*Shit I would have been better off not saying anything and just walking out.*'

"Uh…is…this…room 208?" Sophie finished embarrassed by her failed attempt to look cool. Students in the classroom looked as if they were holding in bundles of laughter.

The room was silent again, for a second or two. Then the teacher spoke, breaking the silence.

"I believe that's what it said outside the door." Sophie heard a few people giggle in the back of the room, others had smiles and grins. The teacher cleared her throat as she grabbed her spectacles reading the clip board to find her name.

"Ah…yes…you must be Sophie Gribsie is that correct?" All Sophie did was shake her head yes as her answer. *I guess I was right on with the schedule. I wonder if I can get my next class right too?'*

"Oh, well perfect, you can have a seat right next to Grear Wentworth." Sophie walked towards the boy the teacher was pointing to in the black top hat with a 3 of clubs stuck to the front of it. The boy cleared his throat,

"I believe you meant Bookie Miss…whatever your name is." Bookie said fixing the collar attached to his white buttoned down shirt. The teacher turned to look at him,

"And I believe you meant Mrs. Mye, Mr. Wentworth." She barked back at him. A few people smiled at her. Bookie rolled his eyes. Sophie observed the classroom which smelled of guts. '*It smells like a fresh swamp in here*' was the first thought that struck Sophie's mind. Sophie dropped her book bag next to the table taking her time sliding into the seat next to Bookie. He studied her for a moment, but didn't say anything; after a few seconds he just turned his attention back to the teacher. Mrs. Mye was a short stoutly woman about 4 feet and 9 inches. Her hair was a brownish grayish. From where Sophie was sitting which was in the back of the room near the corner, looked like she was about 62 years old.

"Shouldn't she be retiring?" Sophie whispered aloud thinking no one would hear her. Bookie heard her and he turned abruptly in his seat to face Sophie.

"You know bitch I was just thinking the same thing."

"Fuck you." Sophie said in a monotone voice.

Her first thought was he wasn't ugly, but he's no Taylor Laughtner. He had black shaggy hair and hazel eyes with a button nose.

This feels so familiar. Oh yes it's from that annoying other dumb kid that was on the bus.

"So you wanna play hard to get? Cuz I'm good at that game." Bookie moved in closer. Sophie scrunched her nose up because of this bad odor Bookie had lingering on him. It smelled like a cheap rip off of Ralph Lauren perfume.

Yep…it's an omen.

"Look kid, what do you want? And you need to back up. Please get out of my face."

"Oh, you're feisty huh? I like feisty females. It gets me off." Bookie said smiling still close to her.

Ew, what a perv. She put her head down after a while. And she wished by now that she had gone to gym instead.

'When The Rain Falls'

Mike Monday

A fter 4th period, Sophie headed off to the cafeteria. She hoped that she saw Ginger or vice versa.

"Hey Sophie! Over here!"

She heard a voice that she could recognize anywhere. Ginger met her half way to the table.

"I was going to look for you, but I couldn't find you and plus I didn't want-

"Oh it's ok." Ginger interrupts Sophie. "It's our first day, so it's no big deal. You wanna come with me to get some food?" Ginger invited her putting down her hair letting it meet her shoulders. Sophie was jealous of Ginger's hair, the way it fell from a perfect pony tail down to tangled brown locks. Sophie wished her hair was as good looking as Ginger's, but she knew it could never be naturally that way. Ginger always got all of the guys to like her and left Sophie behind. And when Ginger would get dumped after the guys had got what they wanted she would go cry back to her. Ginger boasted with excitement about another guy named Drew she had been talking to for a few weeks over the summer. But she didn't seem like she was exclusive with him yet. But Sophie knew it was yet to come before Ginger would tell her about it and brag.

Her clothes always fit and hugged her beautiful figure perfectly. Sophie didn't have a figure like that, she was a little thicker than her. Ginger was thin, pretty, and preppy which was what every guy in the school wants.

"Hey do you have this teacher named Mr. Troy?"

Sophie shook her head gathering a bag of bosco sticks on her tray.

"Oh my gosh he's so hot. I have him for art, and boy I wish I could just be the paint brushes he picks up and holds every time he teaches."

"Hmm, that's nice. What's he look like?"

Ginger blushed and giggled sitting down at the table with Sophie.

"Ok he's tall; he has this to die for killer tan. And oh jeeze, he has the body of a god. His chest is strong; he has these dark chocolate milky eyes and his hair is so dark and silky. Oh and he has this tattoo on the bottom of his wrist."

Sophie smiled. "Well great, now all you have to do is find out his address, his birthday, and his social security number."

Ginger laughed taking a bite of her sandwich. "Don't worry I'll know that by the end of the week, or better yet tomorrow. So, how are your teachers?"

Sophie let out a laugh. "Lame."

Ginger brushed her hair back out of her face letting it fall back down in silky wavy layers. It annoyed Sophie when she did that a lot.

"How so?"

"Well first of all my study hall teacher Ms. Buffit, I swear she's blind as a bat, because these guys were throwing paper at me. And I didn't even know who they were and I told them to stop. So I took one of the pieces of paper they threw at me and I threw it back and I missed. And Ms. Buffit yelled at me and said stop throwing paper. And I tried to tell her the dumb ass boys behind me kept bothering me and I was just throwing it back. And you know what she said?"

"No what?"

"She said she didn't see anything. And I'm like really?

"What? That's so bogus."

"I know I hate that teacher. I'm gonna ask to get my seat changed because I can't stand it."

Ginger shrugged. "Well I like all my teachers, well so far anyway. Especially Mr. Troy. Man if I was old enough I'd marry him."

"Well in some countries that's actually allowed."

"Yeah I know, but I don't think he'd go through all that trouble for us to be together."

"What are you talking about Ginger? He wouldn't go through ANY trouble for you guys to be together."

Ginger laughed. "You don't know him like I do."

"Then I guess I know more than you."

After lunch, Sophie realized Biology class was the only class she got correct. According to the teachers in the other random classes she wasn't suppose to be there. Sophie simply just told them that the office didn't print out her schedule yet but they will do so soon. And the dumb teachers believed her and let her stay.

The next day, Sophie made it on time to Biology class. But today they had a substitute because Mrs. Mye wasn't feeling too well. Sophie sat in the same seat as yesterday; the only thing that was different was that she didn't see Bookie. Sophie glanced up at the clock, watching as the time ticked by. Bookie only had a minute to get there. Unexpectedly, the door opened just as the bell began to ring. Bookie walked into class, still wearing the black top hat with a three of clubs stuck to it. *Man I was hoping he wasn't coming today.*

"Hey bitch." Bookie softly spoke sitting down in his seat.

"Fuck you." Sophie said in monotone.

"So, what's the agenda for today?"

Sophie simply shrugged yawning covering her mouth leaning away from Bookie.

"I think we have a substitute though. So...-

"Where? Where is she?!"

"Um...I thought I saw her a minute ago, maybe she went to the bathroom." Sophie answered him. Suddenly the door crept open again, the substitute walked in. She was wearing a short tight skirt the color of black, with high heels that were way too big for her, and had a gray business buttoned down jacket.

"Ok class," The teacher began, "Since the teacher didn't really leave me with a plan, we're just going to watch a movie."

"What movie is it?" A person sitting in front of the room asked her.

"It's probably nothing good anyways. Do you really think Mrs. Mye would really let us watch something worth watching or interesting?" Bookie spat out. The teacher let out a sigh getting out the cassette tape from teacher's desk as she gave Bookie a glare.

"The movie is called Life." A few people sighed or grunted slouching in their seats. Some put their head down in disgust; others looked bored before the movie started.

"Again? I swear if I ever see this damn movie one more time… I'm gonna literally have no life." Bookie mumbled to himself slouching in the seat. A few people exchanged stares but didn't say anything. The teacher just ignored what was said putting the tape into the VCR. Sophie however, didn't pay attention to the movie; she saw it twice.

Right after the boring class ended, Sophie didn't forget to make her way down the crowded hall ways and stairs to the office. It seemed like she was in a parade and couldn't get out of all the noisy chaos. Some girl walking by talking to her friends had this obnoxious huge PINK bag that wacked Sophie smack dab in the back. Sophie almost fell on the floor but luckily, she caught her balance. After she gathered her composure she turned around to see if she could spot the girl who wacked her. But of course, she couldn't see more than a few feet above all of the sweaty basketball players who were twice her height. *Man, that bitch almost gave me a concussion, if I didn't know any better I'd think I was in a boxing ring in this hall wa-*

Before Sophie could even finish her train of thought some more tall guys walked past her and accidentally pushed her over.

'What the hell?' Sophie dusted herself off once again. She heard the boy's apology faintly echo through all the other noise that was surrounding her. Sophie just forgot about it and made her way to the office. She spotted two women sitting behind a desk. The office smelled like Lysol, but at least it smelled better than the hallway of mess she came from. She noticed someone in the back with a violin softly playing classical music that soothed the atmosphere. Once the two women noticed her walk in, both looked up at the same time. The older woman opened her mouth about to talk when the younger woman interrupted her.

"Yes? Can I help you?" Sophie glanced over to the older woman sitting there and she looked down with a look that said, 'Well I guess ill just shut up then.'

"Yeah um…I'm Sophie Gribsie and I'm here to get my schedule

so could you get it?" Sophie demanded standing there like she had a busy day and some where else important to be. The woman slightly raised her eyebrows at her.

"Well…do you know how to say please and thank you?" She questioned her, putting a cap back on her pen.

"Yeah I know how to say those words I've said them before." Sophie sarcastically smiled at her. The woman didn't take it too kindly.

"Well then now would be a grrreeaat time to use it don't you think?"

"Okay and who are you? Tony the tiger? Look lady I just need my schedule and I can be on my mary way." The woman snickered; the other woman however looked away from the conversation pretending that she wasn't eavesdropping. She held a magazine up to her face to help mask it. Sophie was taken a back at how the woman didn't take her seriously. *What is wrong with this lady? I've been through a hell of a lot of bitches today but she's probably the worst one.* Sophie placed her hand on her hip and began to tap her foot impatiently waiting for the woman to say something. Sophie let out a sigh rolling her eyes as well.

"Well are you gonna get a move on to get my schedule? Or should I just personally go back there and get it myself?"

The woman just gave a pleasant smile. But Sophie could tell that underneath she was cussing her out in her mind which was nothing new on Sophie's behalf.

"I'll get it if you apologize for your beha-

"Ok sorry." Sophie was blunt about it. "There you go, you got your apology, now can you please go get what I asked for now? Appreash." Sophie loved saying the word Appreash which was just an abbreviated phrase from appreciate. She used it as her weapon to get people angry and to annoy them. Sophie gave the lady a fake smile. And once the woman turned around to go get her schedule Sophie's smile twisted upside down into a ugly look. The woman walked back over to the desk and handed Sophie her schedule. She snatched it out of her hand and just walked right out. No one was in the halls anymore except for a few teachers walking to their class rooms. Sophie mumbled under her breath, "Thanks bi-

The classical music used as the passing period bell had let one strong final note out before signaling for the period to start. She opened the piece of paper and there typed was her schedule, the right one. *Hmm…I was sorda right on. I only missed like 6 classes out of the 7 but I still did pretty well.* Sophie folded it and placed it in her pocket.

The next period, Sophie had English class with the teacher Mr. Haiter. Sophie heard of him before, people make fun of his name and call him a hater if he gives them a poor grade on an assignment. Sophie walked in and took a seat in the back of the room. Mr. Haiter noticed her.

"Um…," He walks over to where Sophie was sitting and she looked up at him giving a nasty look like she always gives Bookie when she sees him. The room smelled similar to the way the office did, fresh with a little mixture of the aroma the hall way contained which was sweat.

"Do you have a pass?" Mr. Haiter held his hand out like Sophie was suppose to give him money.

"Does it look like I have a pass?"

"Does it look like I have the patience to put up with your attitude?" He bent over hovering over Sophie's desk to meet her in the eye. Sophie looked at him and shook her head no. Mr. Haiter rose back. He twisted around with his back to Sophie. She flicked him off. A few people in the class room smiled and giggled. Mr. Haiter cleared his throat before speaking.

"Now class," Mr. Haiter began. A few people filed in and sat in front of Sophie. Mr. Haiter looked at them waited till they sat down and continued talking. Sophie's mouth fell open in amazement.

Okay so he doesn't say anything to them who walked in even later than I did, but he'll yell at me? Why does every teacher seem to hate me in this school? They must have formed an "I hate Sophie Gribsie pact" it is unstupidbelieveable. Whatever. Sophie slouched in her seat not wanting to be there at all. The sun shone straight in her eye blinding her and she wished she'd of sat in the front. But then again she'd be closer to the Haiter and she didn't want to be anywhere near him.

"My name is Mr. Haiter," people in the front by the window cut him off with a faint sound of giggles. Mr. Haiter stopped what he was doing abruptly and walked over there towards them. He placed his hands in his suit pockets.

"Is there a problem ladies?"

The girls shook their heads no.

"Then here's what you can do...you can shut your damn mouths and pay attention." Mr. Haiter barked to them. Both girls jumped once he finished his sentence. Mr. Haiter was an alcoholic. And it wasn't that hard to figure out since you could smell the smell of it on his clothes when he walked by, or from a mile away. He never had a clean shave either, and at times he would have trouble keeping his eyes open.

"Now class, as I was saying, welcome to English class. My name is Mr. Haiter. And...hmm...well...I think that's it. Any questions?" The room became silent, and Sophie could swear that she heard crickets in the distance. Mr. Haiter looked around the room at everyone awkwardly, the students, did the same. After a few moments of silence, Mr. Haiter gave them an assignment which was a thick packet. He required them to do 10 pages, or else it would be their first zero they'd ever receive in class. Sophie just knew it was going to be a tough year for her. The teachers were boring, she got too much homework, and the students were weird and uncomfortable, what else could possibly go wrong?

Later on that day, Sophie stayed after school for the informational meeting about the poetry club, her mother texted her telling her she'd be outside waiting for her. Sophie thought that this day couldn't get any worse, her feet hurt from P.E. She was upset that she had to mess up her new gym shoes and she laid her hand on her head. Sophie had an awful headache, and to top things off had a lot of homework. She heard splashing come from within the pool room that was up ahead in the lengthy hallway. Sophie passed by the first time like she wasn't interested, then someone caught her eye.

"Wait a second, who... is that?" Sophie said to herself taking a step backward to glance once again in the poolroom. The air from it was lukewarm against her sweaty sticky skin with a touch of mist every now and then. She saw a well built teenage boy probably a little older than her, and taller than her. This hot hunk, tower of gorgeous guy got out of the pool. He was drenched in water his hair was in strings of gold water dripping down from one strand at a time. But the thing that really got Sophie's attention was his body. He had really cheese grading abs, and a good tan.

I may not of known Mr. Troy, but I don't think his body looks as good as this.

All of the things she saw at once caused Sophie's knees to weaken. He placed a towel on his head and shook it around to dry off. Then, without even expecting it, he looked at Sophie straight through the poolroom opening. His eyes were intense, and oddly it caused Sophie to want to have him, right then and there. She swallowed hard, placing her cold hand on her throat. All she could do was stare at him like an idiot. He gave a whiter than a tooth paste charming smile. Even his smile was as good looking as his body. He wrapped the towel around himself, disappearing into the changing room. She wished she could follow him and see him there, just the thought of it made her want to. Sophie's eyes followed long and hard, and thinking that just seeing this boy made her day a whole lot better, and all he had to do was smile.

Once she got home she had gotten a text from Ginger asking her if she could come and hang out after her ballet practice. She went downstairs to ask her mom but stopped in the middle of stairs to listen in on the argument her parents were having.

"No! I told you to put them in the washer, and what did you do?? Just kept watching the game and eating a bowl of chips like ya always do."

"What? Brenda, come on you know I work hard all day I told you my back was out and my knees hurt."

"Oh! Really?! But they weren't hurting when you went out with your buddies to sit at the bar slouched and drinking."

"It's called having fun, you should try it sometime."

"Terrance I'm really not in the mood to argue, I think your chips are calling you."

"Mom!" Sophie suddenly interrupted and both of her parents abruptly stopped what they were doing.

"Ginger wanted to know if I can go to her ballet practice and then afterwards hang out at the coffee shop."

Her mom let out a sigh placing the basket of laundry down.

"Sure I'll drive you honey because I know SOMEONE else will

be too busy sitting. I'll be back love you."

"Yup you're damn right and love you too." Terrance said sitting down in the recliner.

Brenda backed the car out of the drive way mumbling something under her breath. Sophie looked around the car awkwardly.

"So honey how was your first day?" Brenda's voice trying to sound as calm as possible turning at the end of the block.

"It was…good I guess."

"Make any new friends?"

Sophie laughed. "Trust me mom, I want nothing to do with anyone in that stupid school. Except for…" Sophie remembered the tall handsome young boy she'd seen through the opening of the pool room. Just reminiscing on how hot he made her feel, how weak her knees were, and how much she wanted his attention and affection, and it made her feel like she was reliving that very moment all over again.

"Except for what?" Brenda cut off Sophie's fantasy.

"Oh nothing."

"Hey your dad and I were thinking about taking a quick family trip sometime this year."

"I hope it's not to that dumb water park resort where that kid pushed me in the pool a couple years back."

Brenda laughed. "No no no, it's not that at all we were thinking about you know going camping, or even taking a trip down to your grandpa's ranch in the country side doesn't that sound fun?"

Sophie shrugged, "I guess. Anything's better than that water park."

"And he said you could bring a friend, maybe Ginger would like to come along."

"Yeah maybe."

Brenda pulled up in front of the ballet studio. "I'll call you when I'm ready to be picked up." Sophie closed the car door and rushed inside. She heard a piano being played in the background along with chatter and laughter. Sophie followed the noise and came across a door with a glass window. She peeked through and observed Ginger stretching on the floor and fixing her pink tights. Sophie knocked on the window and she caught Ginger's attention and she ran to the door opening it for Sophie.

"Hey, glad you're here I needed some company." Ginger sat down on the shiny wood floor and continued to stretch. Sophie glanced around the room and saw other ballerinas stretching, practicing leaps, and pirouettes. Most of them looked and stared at Sophie which made her uncomfortable. She saw one of the ballerinas, a tall dark skinned girl, whispering something into one of the other ballerina's ear near by. They both laughed and giggled, but Sophie just rolled her eyes and turned her attention back to Ginger.

"Um, are you sure I'm allowed to be in here?" Sophie asked looking back at the door thinking she would have been better off not showing up.

"Yeah my teacher doesn't care just as long as were not too distracted. I have this recital that I have to perform in a week or so and I'm scared out of my mind. I have trouble with this one leap, and sometimes my partner doesn't show up. It's just a real mess."

Sophie nodded awkwardly placing her hands in her pockets rocking like a rocking chair. "Well you're a good dancer, I'm sure you'll be fine."

"Yeah I guess." Then suddenly the room fell silent, and the playing of the piano filled the room. And in the corner Sophie observed the tall dark skinned ballerina in first position stance with her heels touching and her feet pointed outward. Her knees were perfectly straight with her arms curved bringing her hands into a cradle in front of her sternum. The girl began with a leap, her toes perfectly pointed. She stretched her legs far and wide with each turn and spin she performed. She kept spinning and spinning all the way to where Ginger and Sophie were gathered. The girl stopped for a split moment and gave Sophie a glare, and then kicked her leg out straight and leaped away across the other side of the room. All you could hear were her gracious smooth footsteps gliding across the floor. She descended down in perfect harmony with the music of *Swan Lake* from the piano, wrapping her arms gently around herself. Everyone immediately clapped, and neither Sophie nor Ginger noticed the teacher standing in the doorway and she came rushing up to the girl and gave her a warm embrace.

"Bravo, that was wonderful Somone, you never make me regret

telling everyone I know that you're one of the best dancers I've had, let's all give her another round of applause." And the room once more filled with claps and compliments. Both Sophie and Ginger stuck out like a sore thumb because they didn't look impressed, and they didn't bother clapping. Ginger stood up and went to go and snatch her satchel in the far corner of the room and she left with Sophie following right behind.

"Gosh I hate her so much. She annoys the shit out of me." Ginger looked at herself in the mirror in the hallway brushing her brown curly hair. She slammed her brush down on the table taking out her chap stick.

"I could tell."

"Like it's so annoying she always gets all the compliments, the teacher just looooves her. And she's considered to be one of the "best" dancers? That's a bunch of bull shit." Ginger's face was a fainted red as she placed her curly locks into a messy bun. "Let's get out of here." She said through gritted teeth slamming all of her belongings in her satchel and hurrying out into the sun set. Once they reached the coffee shop they ordered mocha frappes and sat down at a table near a window.

"So what's up?" Ginger asked crossing her legs setting her satchel on the table.

Sophie shrugged, "Nothing really just you know, the usual."

Ginger smiled leaning back in her chair.

"It's always the usual with you, you hardly ever tell me about any guy trouble, or any drama going on."

Sophie looked down and blushed, "Well…"

Ginger leaned forward in her seat strings of her hair falling from the tangled bun.

"Well what?"

"There is this one guy…" Sophie smiled to herself still not making eye contact.

"Oh really? What's his name?"

It wasn't apparent to Sophie until now, but she never really thought about his name. It shocked her that she didn't think about it before.

"I…don't know what his name is."

"What? How could you not know his name?"

"I don't know I mean…"

"Well where did you meet him?"

Sophie took a long drink of her frappe wondering if she should have just kept her mouth shut. Her eyes darting from one side of the coffee shop to the other.

"Well…I didn't exactly meet him…I just saw him, and he saw me."

"So basically…you know nothing about him?" Ginger took her hair down brushing it back with her fingers.

"I know he has a nice body."

Ginger laughed. "How do you know?"

"I saw it…" Sophie answered her voice growing quiet.

"Where exactly did you see this guy?"

"It was after school, and you know that pool room in that long hallway near the English rooms?"

Ginger nodded her head.

"Well I saw him in the pool, he was swimming and…then he caught me staring and he looked at me and smiled. And oh my gosh let me tell you, he had a nice tan, nice abs, and smile and everything. I just wanted to die in those arms of his."

"Wow Sophie I've never seen you like this before."

"What do you mean?"

"I mean I've never seen you all head over heels in love with someone."

Sophie almost chocked on her frappe. "What? I never said I was in love with him. I just think he's attractive. That's all." She shrugged trying to make herself believe what came out of her own mouth. But she had a feeling they both knew it was a lie.

"Is he on the swim team?"

"Hm…I don't know, I'm guessing so."

Ginger leaned forward even more slamming her hand down on the table and gasped with excitement.

"If he is you should go to one of his competitions."

"What?"

"Yeah! That'd be a great idea, and then you have an excuse to talk to him."

"What am I gonna say? He probably already thinks I'm weird."

"Why would he think that?"

"Well let's see because he was just minding his own business and there I am like an idiot staring at him. Wouldn't that freak you out?"

"Well it obviously didn't freak him out if he smiled at you. I still think you should go to one of his swimming competitions though seriously."

"Well what about you? How's that guy Drew?" Sophie tried to change the subject.

"Oh he's good, I was texting him the other day and he wanted to hang out this weekend or something."

Sophie nodded.

"But he hasn't asked me out or anything. But I really like him and he's really nice." Ginger smiled and looked out the window, her hazel eyes glistening into the fading light. She took a sigh.

"But something just seems different about him you know? But I'm nervous because I think he's into me but I'm not sure because when I'm with him he sends me signals that he likes me but he hasn't asked me out. I know! Maybe this weekend or next weekend or something you could meet him and tell me what you think of him."

Sophie looked down at her cup picking at the wrapping from around her frappe buying time thinking of what to say.

"Um...I have to see if I'm available."

Ginger smiled. "Terrific I'll text you and let you know."

The next day, Sophie was in the lunch line waiting for the lunch lady at the cashier to count all of the pennies this boy had laid down in front of her. Some people behind her were too impatient to wait and started eating some of their lunch in line. Sophie figured she might as well just eat some of her bosco sticks because the line didn't seem like it was gonna move any time soon.

Oh shoot, I really wanted some of those double chocolate cookies. Luckily one of Ginger's friends Maggie was behind her.

"Hey Maggie, you mind saving my spot real quick? I forgot to go grab something."

Maggie pulled Sophie's tray closer to hers and continued talking to Ginger behind her. Sophie weaved in and out through the crowded area like a salmon moving up stream over to the basket of fresh baked cookies. A lunch lady walked over with a tray and scrapped some fresh ones into the basket. She turned to Sophie and gave her a warm smile.

Yes just in time for some fresh ones. Sophie heard a group of guys walk in and join the crowd but she was too focused on which cookie she had a craving for.

Hmmmm...should I get the double chocolate cookie, or the M&M cookie?

She could feel someone beside her waiting so she quickly made up her mind grabbing four double chocolate cookies about to place them on her tray but something made her look up. And from the moment her knees went weak, her body grew still, and her heart beat echoed through her ears she saw the same charming smile and those daring blue eyes only this time up close.

"Hey Slyder could you pass me some ketchup?!" Sophie heard a guy say from across the room. She saw Slyder grab a packet and chuck it.

"Thanks man."

Slyder turned his attention back to her and Sophie's hand that held the tongs began to tremble.

Fuck, shit shit damn damn damn! "Hey Ginger uh...I...I got your cookies!" Sophie yelled throwing the cookies on her tray. Ginger turned to her as Sophie began placing the cookies in her hand one by one.

"What are you talking about?" Ginger said confused looking down at the stack of cookies in her hand.

"Just play along." Sophie's teeth stuck together being discreet.

Now I know I have no chance talking to him. Shit! Why did I do that??? Why??

Sophie looked petrified joining Ginger and the rest of her friends at the lunch table. All of them were talking about papers they had to write, and of course boys they liked that don't even notice their existence. But Sophie was still caught up in her own thoughts. She thought about turning around just one quick second to see if he was still there. She could feel her body about to do it, but it was like a strong force was stopping her. She wished the force that stopped her now had stopped her sooner maybe it could have saved her from the embarrassment.

"Yeah," Ginger rang her voice a loud, "The teachers here are so stupid, and I mean like I know they give us homework for practice. But where does resting like ever come in? Oh and here you go." Ginger placed the four cookies on Sophie's tray.

"I want to have kids when I grow up." A girl named Mallory announced, as a dreamy feature came across her face, her eyes looking up at the ceiling. Sophie gazed away from the table as the girls kept their discussion going. Sophie took notice of the group of guys from the lunch line walk past the table. You could always tell when Slyder was about to walk in a room or down a hallway. There would always be a gaper's gap. Girls from left and right would stand there and gawk at him. He was wearing a pure white tank top that hugged his figure exposing his killer six pack that rippled underneath. He was the first boy that Sophie saw who didn't wear jeans that were around their ankles or baggy. Whenever she laid her eyes on his luscious hot body he made her feel lust, important, and down right sexy. She stared intensely at him, watching as he passed their table. The smell of his cologne lingered in the air, and Sophie loved it.

"Sophie? Hello?" Ginger said to her waving a hand in front of her face.

"Huh? What?"

"Were you listening to what I said?" Ginger asked her. Sophie shook her head no, and not even then, she still wasn't paying attention. She spotted the tower of gorgeous sitting socializing with his friends. Suddenly, Sophie saw him stand up from the table and strolled over to the vending machine and she checked him out as he went. She saw him pull a wallet out of his jeans back pocket. After that, all she saw was his back and him gathering some money out. She thought about going up to him, but hesitated. She stood up easing her way over to him. She felt like a robot, her movements not her own. Sophie continued to approach him, not caring if she embarrassed herself a second time.

He tore open a candy wrapper looking eagerly to satisfy a sweet tooth. And Sophie just stood there like a lost puppy thinking that even if he didn't turn around, she was content with just seeing his back. It still would have been nice to be looked at with those sinful, yet innocent piercing blue eyes. Eyes that were overflowing with mysteriousness, anger, and hate, yet benevolent and soothing intentions. He walked away from her leaving her there like an idiot. She dug around in her pocket and pulled out 50 cents. She turned and faced the display of candy. There was rows of M&M's, Hershey, Peanut Butter Cup, and Snickers, all decked out for her. She figured since she was up there she might as well just buy something. Sophie saw a Hershey Bar and she had a craving. Sophie placed her 25 cents in one at a time. She had the other quarter in her hand about to place it in the change slot when Bookie approached her frightening her causing her to jump up. The quarter fell out of her hand rolling its way under the machine.

"Damn it Bookie!"

He gave a grin. He was watching Sophie bend down on the ground with her butt sticking straight up in the air trying to retrieve the quarter that had fallen out of her grasp. After a few failed attempts, she accepted that it was out of her reach. And Sophie observed that her quarter had joined a couple other quarters that probably ended up there the same way hers had. Bookie switched from beside Sophie to behind her.

"Man, I love this view." Bookie told Sophie moving in closer to her behind thrusting his hips forward and Sophie stood up.

"Fuck you." Sophie said in a monotone voice. "You owe me a quarter." She ordered. Bookie gave an amazed look like the statement wasn't true. "That's it? No how are you? No what's up or anything?"

"No."

"I see you're still feisty. This just keeps gettin' better and better. Cuz you know what the girls say about me? I'm a fox sly and quick."

Sophie looked at him like he was stupid. "Well sorry but I'm not one those dumb girls you hang around with. Now give me my damn quarter or pay for the candy yourself." Bookie let out a laugh.

"You really seem to think it's gonna be that easy."

She raised her eyebrows at him. She grabbed his collar of his shirt and forced him against the wall.

"Oh," Bookie moaned deeply. "Throw me around some more. I like that."

"Hey you know what why don't you do me a favor and get another quarter? How bout that?"

Bookie shrugged. "Well I don't know…depends what you were gonna buy." Bookie grinned.

"I was gonna eat a Hershey Bar."

"Well then maybe I can eat you."

"Give…me…my…quarter."

Bookie threw both hands up and surrendered. "Alright alright chill." He dug around in his pants pocket and gave her a quarter. "There. Ya happy?"

Sophie snatched the quarter out of Bookie's hand and bought the Hershey Bar she'd been craving.

"Hey uh…I'm having this party, wanna go?"

Sophie didn't answer him right away. She took her time opening her chocolate bar wrapper and took a bite of it.

"Well I don't know…I'm probably gonna be busy. So…"

"Well…it's on Friday if you wanna come."

"Who else is going?" Sophie asked him.

"All the cheerleaders, the football players, the soccer players, uh… hmm…and um…a couple other people from a different school are going too."

"What time does it start?"

Bookie smiled at her moving in closer to her backing her into the corner. Sophie gave him a nasty look.

"Once the sun goes down baby." He answered her.

"Uh ok, and never call me that again."

"Sorry." Bookie apologized backing up letting Sophie slip away.

Chapter Three

"Do you have a Pixel me account?" Ginger asked Sophie, clicking and typing on the computer.

"No, what's that?" Ginger giggled a bit; she swirled around in her computer chair to face Sophie who was lying across her bed staring at the ceiling bored out of her mind.

"I can't believe you've never heard of it, I think almost everyone has one."

Sophie rolled her eyes.

"Well what is it?" Sophie irritatingly asked once more. Ginger turned back around.

"Come over here I'll show you."

Sophie sluggishly got up and walked over towards the computer where Ginger was sitting. She stood there and crossed her arms.

"It looks like any other website." Sophie stated not sounding impressed.

"But it's fun though; do you want me to make you an account?"

"Sure, why not?" Sophie announced walking back over to the bed and sitting there once again.

"Are you planning on going to Bookie's party this Friday?" Ginger was trying to make conversation. Sophie simply shrugged.

"I don't know I don't really wanna to go. Bookie creeps me out."

"Oh come on, he's a really sweet guy. He added me on Pixel."

"Well if you want a creeper for a friend then that's all you."

"Oh come on Sophie, he's just trying to be friendly he's not all that bad." Ginger defended him. Sophie let out a long sigh.

"He scared me the other day at the vending machine. Didn't you see him?" Ginger shook her head no as a response.

"Well... he did." It was silent for a moment. "Are you going?" Sophie added. She heard Ginger giggle a bit still typing on the computer.

"Of course I am silly, why wouldn't I be going?"

"Well I hope you have fun without me." Sophie twisted and turned in the tangled mess on the bed.

"I promise I'll be with you the whole time, I wont ditch you like I did last time I promise, just please just go everyone's going to be there."

"Well what about you and that Drew guy? Weren't you supposed to see him this weekend or something?"

Ginger shook her head. "No that's probably gonna be next week. And guess what."

"Hm?"

"He asked me out."

Sophie sat up on the bed. "What did you say?"

Ginger shrugged sitting at the edge of the bed next to Sophie.

"I told him that…I have to think about it. And he said ok. But I still want you to meet him anyway. Speaking of guys, any update with yours?"

Sophie smiled shyly and turned on her stomach twirling the loose yellow knitting on the blanket around her index finger. "Yeah, I know what his name is. But just his first name though."

"And?" Ginger squealed sitting Indian style.

"His name is Slyder."

"Wait Slyder? Slyder Thomas?"

"You know him?"

"Well no…I think Drew's friend is friends with him. But I've heard of him before. But yeah I heard that he's a hard catch."

Sophie laughed. "It doesn't matter to me one way or the other, I already knew that there would never be a him and I."

"But how do you know that?"

"Well because…I mean…guys like Slyder Thomas go for girls like…Taylor Windowski, or Molly Fritter, or even that girl Sarah North Face with the big boobs."

They both laughed.

"That's not even her name is it?" Ginger asked.

"No, it's just people call her that because she gets a new North Face jacket every day with new Uggs and that ugly PINK brand all the girls like."

"Hey some of PINK'S products are cute; I have a few of their sweat pants but they're expensive."

"Yeah I saw how much they cost; I wouldn't pay that much for a pair of sweat pants."

"Why don't you just give it a shot? And besides all those girls are taken."

"Well that doesn't mean they don't want Slyder as much as I do. I mean…"

"Ha! So, you do like him then." Ginger smiled.

"Well duh. I mean no I mean whatever you know what I meant. And Taylor Windowski, Molly Fritter, and Sarah North Face are only taken on school days."

Ginger cracked up laughing. "Don't they date each other's boyfriends?"

"Yeah they pass them around like little hand me down shirts or something. But hey I mean…it seems to work for them so…whatever."

They both laughed and Sophie's stomach began to hurt.

"You're gonna make me pee on myself." Ginger laughed some more.

"Well you and me both."

"Well tomorrow the boys swim team has their first competition of the season."

"So?" Sophie said turning over on her back.

"So Slyder's gonna be there."

"And you know this how?"

"Because Drew's friend's friend met Slyder in swimming. So that's gotta mean something, right?"

"Sophie your mother is outside waiting for you." Ginger's mother wiped some paint on her smock.

"Ok thanks Mrs. Spring I'll be right out."

Mrs. Spring smiled closing the bedroom door. Sophie turned her attention back to Ginger. "Anyway, I'll see you tomorrow."

"Wait but come to the swimming competition with me."

"But why?"

"Pleeeaaaasssseee." Ginger placed both hands together begging Sophie. Sophie stood there beside the bed, wondering just how far she could project into the future and have her predictions be right. Was this Slyder Thomas really worth all this fuss over? All this guessing, all this worrying, or even all this talking? What if Ginger was right? Her words went through Sophie's head once more 'I heard he's a hard catch.' But was he too much of a hard catch? Even for Sophie's ability? She honestly didn't think she had what it took to be with him, to be considered his girlfriend, let alone even talk to him. With all of his wide variety of girls he could choose, why would Sophie even be included in it anyway? She inhaled a deep breath, trying to calm herself down from all the negativity.

"Ok fine." Sophie said plainly. And immediately Ginger rushed over to her squealing like she always does when she's excited.

"Great, I'll see you tomorrow then."

Red blazers, red skirts, white shirts and red pants were all Sophie saw walking the hallways of Vermyear Academy. Sometimes the students were given free days also known as casual day where the students got to wear whatever they wanted which most of them never chose to wear their uniforms. To Sophie, the uniforms were hideous. The girls had to wear red skirts that reached half way down their thighs along with white tops that mostly hugged their outline. Some girls wore white stockings because they hated exposing their legs along with black high heel shoes. As for the guys, they had to wear white button down shirts, with red pants, black shoes and red blazers. Sophie didn't like how everyone she passed looked the same as the other people that she passed before.

Ugly, ugly ugly ugly…ugh even uglier. Sophie thought as she passed person after person giving them all nasty glares. She saw one girl walk passed her with mixed matched stockings, one green and one purple. *Oh, my gosh…what is happening to our species?* Sophie was on her way to her French class. She was always intrigued on learning a second language. She sat where she usually sat in all her other classes which was in the back row. She looked towards the door to see who was coming in but it wasn't really anyone she recognized except Bookie.

Oh, my gosh…please don't come over here and talk to me please don't.'

Bookie noticed her and began to make his way through several students.

No no no turn around please turn around don't come over here.

"Hey good lookin'." Bookie slid down in the seat right next to Sophie. She laid her hand on her head like she had a headache.

"Oh, aren't you gonna call me a bitch?"

"Alright…Hey bitch."

"Fuck you…and what the hell do you want?" Sophie spoke from underneath her breath.

"You know what I want." Bookie scooted his seat along close to Sophie's desk.

"Why are you in almost every single one of my classes?" Sophie's voice rose with each scoot Bookie's chair made. He sat there pondering about it for a second.

"Hm…I don't know, maybe its fate." Bookie said with a smile. A sudden shadow glided over them which caused them both to look up to see that it was. The teacher, who was towering over them, had black hair pulled back in a pony tail with a brown suit. She peered and looked at Bookie.

"Are you Mr. Grear Wentworth?" The teacher's voice was stern and serious. Bookie stood up right away and popped up his collar trying his best to look impressive.

"Yes, that's me, but you can call me Bookie, Miss." He held out his hand wanting to give her a hand shake. The teacher turned her nose up at it. She looked down at her clip board with hugging arms but didn't bother giving Bookie a hand shake.

"Well Mr. Grear Wentworth you sit all the way over there." She pointed to the other side of the room scribbling something down on her clip board. Bookie took a sigh and walked away from the teacher and Sophie. Sophie was relieved he was gone and the teacher watched him go then turned to face Sophie.

"And are you Sophie Gribsie?" Sophie nodded her head yes.

"Well you sit two seats up." Sophie dragged her belongings on the ground and sat where she was told. She heard the teacher tell someone to sit behind her, but Sophie didn't bother to turn around because she had an awful crook in her neck from sleeping wrong the other night. Once the teacher seated everyone in their assigned seats, she walked over to the chalk board and picked up a small piece of chalk.

"Good afternoon, and welcome to French class. My name is Ms. Pompe. Say that with me, Pompe," The class said her name with her in unison. "Good very good. The first thing I'm going to hand out to you is this sheet that tells you the rules of the classroom." Ms. Pompe gathered a stack of papers and began handing them out to the first person in each row. The person in front of Sophie passed it back to her and she turned to pass the paper back to the person behind her. But once she did, she froze. The guy leaned forward in his seat and grabbed the paper that was in Sophie's hand.

"Thank you." His voice was sweet like chocolate mousse.

"Sophie, Slyder, is there a problem?" The teacher asked standing in front of the classroom waiting for them to give her their full attention. Before Sophie could even open her mouth to speak, Slyder stepped in.

"No sorry, it was my fault." The teacher gave a stern look.

"Well just don't let it happen again." Sophie turned around to face the front where the teacher was.

"Now class, if you read these rules they will be very helpful to you because I take these rules very seriously. You can just ask any of my other students I have had. Alrighty," The teacher clapped her hands together. "I'm sure probably most of you don't know anything about French except how to say hello right?" A few people in the class nodded their heads in agreement. The teacher passed out another sheet of paper welcoming the class and it had a list of needed supplies. She also gave them a pop quiz on the French language to assess their knowledge. The teacher allowed the students to pack up early before the bell rang and Sophie felt compelled to steal a glance at Slyder, but she didn't want to. She felt like an addict.

There probably is a rehab treatment out there to weene all of the junkies off of all the "Slyder Thomas' in the world. I should ask the counselor.

Even when he wasn't there, he was always on her mind even before they started talking for the first time. He had that effect on her, made her do what he wanted, say what he wanted, look at him the way he wanted, and feel the way he wanted. He made her feel nervous and excited, tense and loose, and desired. She kept her eye on the clock pleading for the bell to ring; they weren't even serious, they were barely even friends and already she's stressing over him. It drove her crazy. Sophie couldn't stand it. She couldn't hold on anymore. She needed her fix. She looked over and was immediately succumbed by his intense concentration. His eyes were so passionate.

OMFG...DAMN! I cannot believe that someone could make me act this insane. I mean, there are a million guys in this school. How did I get in this mess? But I mean...look at those deep eyes, and strong hands. You can almost feel them. Penetrating. Sophie leaned in to get a better look at what Slyder was so mesmerized by. She read:

She, is as beautiful as a rose
She can be as beautiful as anything I suppose
Her smile, oh so bright
She's the sun that brightens the night
I see her and she sees me
Our love will reach the deepest sea
Her skin is like the newest silk, soft and fresh
I was close to her today and I felt her breath
On the side of my face
And stole an embrace
A moment so kind
I will never find
A love as pure and warm
As the form
I held today

Sophie was shocked, she never expected him to be so deep. *Oh, my gosh...This is better, than anything I've ever read from Shakespeare, Poe, and Steinbeck.*

"S s s so you like poetry?" Sophie stuttered, embarrassing herself. *Damn.*

Slyder smiled and stopped with his writing.

"Yeah I write it all the time. Do you?" He began to put his things away in his book bag.

"I I um I don't know how to write."

He responded, "Oh..." As if saying 'how did your illiterate self make it to high school?'

Before Sophie could regain her composure, the bell rang. Sophie met up with Slyder out in the hallway after class and began walking with him.

He was her ultimate fix to her obsessive addiction. A dream that she didn't want to wake up from. He was the doorway to her feelings, to the true Sophie. He was the only one who had the key. She just wasn't sure about anything quite yet. But what she was sure of was that she, Sophie Gribsie, was painfully, unbearably, and foolishly consumed by him.

Sophie was sitting on the steps in front the main entrance of the school waiting for Ginger to arrive. She pulled out her phone checking the time when Ginger came running up to her.

"Hey." Ginger said smiling pushing up her bra under her gray thinned shirt, and pulled down her blue jean shorts from rising up between her thighs. "How do I look?" She asked posing like a runway model.

"Um...great but...isn't it a little chilly out?"

Ginger laughed. "No, it's not too chilly, come on let's go we gotta get a good seat." They both rushed inside meeting all of the chatter and splashing of water once they entered the pool room opening. Sophie saw guys in speedos practicing laps in the pool and stretching getting prepared for the big competition.

"Come on I see a couple seats." Ginger dashed up through the bleachers stepping over woman's bags and purses. She accidentally stepped on a couple people's feet. "Sorry." Ginger quickly said as her and Sophie plopped down onto the metal bleachers. Ginger took out her makeup bag taking out a small hand held mirror and some red lipstick. She placed another heavy coat of it on her lips then rubbed her lips together and brushed her curly hair back with her fingers. "Hey, look you see that guy right there?" Ginger pointed over a couple people's head straight ahead to a boy with stringy black hair stretching by the pool edge.

"Yeah what about him?"

"That's Drew's friend that's friends with Slyder, but I don't see him anywhere. Maybe he's in the back or something." Ginger said clasping her mirror with blush together.

Sophie glanced around the room and saw Cassandra Reese, the one that pushed her down on the ground the first day of school, walk in with her possey. Taylor Windowski, Molly Fritter, and Sarah North Face all filed in after her carrying PINK and Juicy Couture purses.

"Oh, gosh look, it's the three bitches and their walking STD leader." Sophie nudged Ginger in her side.

"Where?"

"Right there." Sophie pointed.

"Really? Why are they here?"

Sophie shrugged noticing all four of them came and sat down diagonal right behind them.

"You see how they just had to sit behind us?" Ginger leaned over and whispered.

"Hey Taylor, did you bring my PINK perfume and my lotion?" Molly asked digging around in her purse.

"Um...Oh sorry, I think I left it in my car." Taylor apologized zipping her purse back.

"It's fine."

"Hey look ladies. There he is, my future boyfriend." Cassandra whispered to all of them. And all of them squealed like scared little piglets. Sophie looked to see who they were speaking of and saw Slyder come from out of the changing room area beside the bleachers heading over to the pool.

"Ah just look at that body. You think he has a nice package?" Sarah asked.

"Hey, he's mine ok? So, don't get too crazy over him." Cassandra stepped in flipping her black hair with her bracelets clanging together. "And besides, from this view it looks like he has more than a good one." Cassandra added and they all laughed. "Hey, is my push up working?" She asked Taylor and she gave a thumbs up.

"Yeah they are."

"Good," Cassandra began checking one more time making sure her boobs looked like baked muffin tops out of her shirt. "Once Slyder sees these I know he won't be able to resist me."

"Did you hear these trailer skanks?" Sophie whispered into Ginger's ear.

"Yeah, they all probably wanna bang him like they did every other guy in this school." Then finally they heard the intercom come on and a loud mans voice began to speak and all of the chatter began to dwindle and die down under his overpowering voice.

"Ladies and Gentlemen, welcome to our first competition of the season. How bout we give all these talented swimmers a round of applause because they all and I mean all of them practiced very very hard." The room filled with an applause and some people in the stands stood up to show their gratitude. "Now," The loud speaker began, "Without further ado let us begin this competition between Vermyear Academy high and St. Langstons." The room filled with an applause once more. The swimming coaches from each school brought their team into a huddle to pep them up to compete. And once each huddle broke loose some of the boys from each side took their places at the edge of the pool doing some last minute stretches and hunched over to take a starting position.

"I see Jeremy. He's so fast just watch how fast this kid is." Ginger whispered into Sophie's ear. She saw a man calmly walk up beside the edge of the pool with a whistle around his neck. He placed it up to his lips and gave it a short blow right away. And immediately the boys pushed off all in perfect timing. Ginger kept her eye on Jeremy and saw that he glided through the water passed every swimmer and hit the other end first making his way back the quickest.

"Whoa did you see that?" Ginger pointed, her words a little drowned out by all the cheering and chatter. The next group of boys had done the same thing but it looked like, from Sophie's point of view, it was a tie. Group after group kept doing the same thing, until she heard people in the stands saying it was the last group to go and right now it was a tie between the two schools. Sophie really wasn't paying attention, she was hot in the humid room, tired from all the cheer, and tired from sitting down in these uncomfortable bleachers. She took out her phone and saw that it was almost 9:00 o'clock.

Come on hurry up and end already. Then Sophie noticed Slyder standing up, which made her pay more attention without any hesitation. She saw his coach talking to him in the corner right before the last set of boys took their places, pumping him up to be ready.

"Wooo go Slyder baby!" Cassandra yelled out in the quiet crowd drawing attention to herself a few women in the front row turned and stared. The boys took their spots in the lanes waiting for the last and final whistle. The whistle blew suddenly, causing the boys to rush into the water. Sophie kept a close eye on Slyder and saw him slither through the water effortlessly and easily neck and neck with another competitor. But Slyder got ahead once they reached the end of the pool and turned to the other side. It seemed like Slyder had picked up a faster pace, slithering even faster and faster until his hand touched the end of the pool ending the race and the competition with a final score.

The crowd suddenly began to cheer and whistle most of them standing up giving a round of applause.

"Yeah see? That's my boyfriend." Cassandra boasted.

"I thought you said he was your future one though..." Molly added confused.

"Oh, whatever I consider him mine. He gave me a wink today in the library it was so hot." Cassandra bragged and boasted some more. A few people in the crowd stood up right away to meet the competitors they were cheering for and a few of the swimmers came to them.

"Come on I wanna see if we can find Jeremy." Ginger said getting up rushing down the bleachers over to a crowd of boys. Ginger ran up to Jeremy, pushing past a couple people, jumping on him giving him a hug. Sophie slowly approached the crowd looking at her phone pretending to be busy.

I'm just gonna stare at my phone the entire time and act like I'm checking a text message or a missed call. She turned around because she heard Cassandra squealing her butt off and saw that she was all over Slyder giving him hugs and occasionally touching his stomach.

"You were fantastic Slyder. And you swam so fast. Did you hear me cheering??" Cassandra said all in his personal space. Between Ginger flirting with the group of swimmers, and Cassandra all over Slyder, Sophie didn't know what to do or where to go. True she was still staring down at her phone the whole time, but even that wasn't making the situation more bearable.

"Hey where are you going Sly?"

Sophie heard Cassandra say behind her.

Sly?? Really? She's giving him nick names now?

"Hey."

Sophie heard a voice say behind her and she twirled around.

"H...h..hi..." She stuttered her response looking at the tangled dripping gold, and those nice abs.

Slyder gave her that charming smile of his she adored so much. "I didn't expect to see you here."

"I....I...didn't either I mean I was just here with Ginger and she wanted me to come and I wasn't sure and she came here for Jeremy and I'd know you'd do great I would have cheered for you but you did good anyway." Sophie ranted on senselessly. *Shit I knew I should have just duck taped my mouth shut. I'd be better off just playing dead.*

All Slyder did was give a smile. "I see... well I'll see ya tomorrow alright?" He gave a smile once more before walking away and Sophie's eyes followed him watching him long and hard.

"Don't...get any ideas." Cassandra told Sophie crossing her arms.

"And who are you to tell me what to do?" Sophie shot at her.

"I'm Slyder's woman, that's who I am."

"I would feel sorry for him even if that was true."

"Look hun, all were saying is to stay away from him unless you want us to beat your ass." Molly stepped in.

"OOOO look at you guys. You guys are still the same ol' crazy psycho bitches I met a long time ago."

"And you're just a bitch." Taylor chimed in.

"You guys must be drinking from the same stupid juice if you think I'm ever gonna listen to either one of you. Now move...preash." Sophie pushed passed breaking through them and headed into the bathroom in the hall. She didn't know why she came in there to begin with, but it was better than staying in that humid room arguing with Cassandra. The door opened and Ginger stumbled in, her hair was a mess and her lipstick smeared.

"Hey, what are you doing in here?" Ginger panted.

Sophie shrugged. "I just wanted to get some air."

Ginger panted some more patting her tangled loose strands down in the mirror. "Wasn't that a great game? Aren't you glad you came along?"

"Yeah until slutty Cassandra and her crew showed up."

"Oh my gosh I know! Did you hear her talking about Slyder like that?"

"Yeah she told me that don't get any ideas because she's his woman. It's like Cassandra...you're only like...sixteen years old like... what are you doing?"

Ginger laughed faintly through her panting. "Right? I'm sick of stupid people."

Sophie laughed. "All people annoy me until I get to know them, and most the time they annoy me even more."

Ginger smiled wiping off the smeared lip stick with a piece of toilet paper. "Let's go." She said tossing the red stained paper in the trash.

Meanwhile, Brenda was relaxing in the recliner giving herself a pedicure. She placed a pair of cucumbers on her eyes snuggled into the sinking chair. She heard Terrance walk in the room plop on the sofa turning the television on and placed his feet on the glass table turning up the volume.

"Hey honey could you turn that down please?"

Terrance took a dramatic sigh barely reducing the noise.

"And could you please not put your feet up on the table I just cleaned that."

Terrance took a long sigh again taking one foot down at a time.

"Thanks, oh and could you also make sure the dishes are clean? I was gonna make dinner tonight."

"Can't you do it when you're done with whatever you're doing?"

Brenda took a sigh placing the cucumbers on the night stand beside her.

"No because my toes will still be drying."

"So?"

"So, I don't wanna mess them up, can't you just please do it for me?"

"You're not gonna use your toes to make sure the dishes are clean are you?"

Brenda stared at him and Terrance did the same, he didn't look like he was going to budge.

"I guess you just expect me to do EVERYTHING around here, while you just sit."

"No not everything, just some things...while I sit."

"Oh my gosh you know what? You're just so damn lazy. Your mother said you were the exact same way when you were younger."

"Yeah but that didn't stop you from marrying me." Terrance's cell phone began vibrating cutting off the argument. "Hello?" "Ok, I'll be right there." "Alright bye."

"And where do you think you're going?" Brenda folded her arms, about to get out of the recliner but remembered her feet were soaking. "I'm going to pick up Sophie I'll be back."

'In For The Kill'

La Roux (Scream Remix)

Cecil and Issac. The palest of all pale people in the world. They're the cold shadow in a dark alley, a chill up your spine, the ugly face in the looking glass. No one in Vermyear Academy took them too kindly. Cecil, unlike any other girl in the school, asked for the longest red skirt the school carried. They would give stares left and right to anyone and everyone. They were always together and never apart. They walked into the lunchroom and looked to see if they could give anyone any unwanted advice about what they should and shouldn't do. They found their perfect pray going in for the kill over to this couple in the corner making out. Cecil and Issac approached them.

"You really shouldn't think about having sex until marriage." Cecil advised. The couple stopped making out and looked at her.

"We didn't ask you." The girl said angrily.

"Why the hell are you over here?" The guy yelled.

"You really shouldn't raise your vo-

"And you really shouldn't get in our business." The girl cut her off adding more anger to her tone. Cecil and Issac never argued. They say what they have to say to you then walk away leaving you no time to respond.

"It's ok Cecil, they're gonna go to hell anyway." Issac said calmly taking Cecil's frail hand and leading her away from the angry couple. They looked for someone else to bother, walking passed Sophie's table over by the window. Ginger stared as they went.

"Man, they're weird." Ginger whispered to Sophie.

"Yeah I know." Sophie looked back over her shoulder at Cecil and Issac who were saying grace before eating their meal.

"They creep me out. I've never seen anyone that pale before in my life. They look like they don't get a lot of sunlight and they always bother people. All the time. I think they just do it to get a thrill out of it or something." Ginger observed.

Cecil and Issac never bought school lunch; they would always bring their own. It was usually bizarre foods that no one in the school would eat, like tofu and cucumber sandwiches and apple juice. Cecil placed her lunch bag on the table and Issac unwrapped her sandwich from the plastic placing it in front of her and Cecil did the same. Issac made sure that each one of Cecil's bleached blonde strands was perfectly curved into her bob hair do. They continued tending to each other like monkeys picking off bugs from one   another.

"Oh Issac, all these people in this lunch room will never understand the importance of life."

"I know my love, but don't worry they'll soon learn. After all, ignorance is expensive, they don't know any better." Issac insisted.

"Now come on Miss. Abola. You really don't wanna give me a D- now do you? I mean come on now. How can you give a D- I mean look at me. Do I look like I'm worth a D-?" Bookie pleaded. Miss. Abola turned to look at him.

"Yeah you're right; I don't wanna give you a D-." Miss. Abola walked back to Bookie's desk. She turned the piece of paper to face her taking her red pen out from behind her ear and crossed out the D- and replaced it with a huge F.

"There, that should work out fine." Miss. Abola continued walking around the class passing students back their tests. Bookie snatched his test off the desk.

"Wait! Ok! Miss. Abola I'll take the D-! Please give me a D-. I don't wanna fail Geometry please!" Miss. Abola ignored his plead still passing papers out. When Sophie got her paper back, she saw that her grade was a C-. She was never good with numbers and Geometry was her weakest subject. But at least she was better than Bookie. Slyder received his paper, and Sophie saw that he got an A+.

Ohh still as hot as ever...I just want him to hold me in those strong tanned arms. That's all I need to keep warm in the winter.

"Miss Abola please please please!! I'm begging you like a dog! I really don't want an F!" Bookie continued pleading and begging but it wasn't giving him any luck. Miss. Abola made her decision. When Bookie realized his begging wasn't going to change Miss. Abola's mind, he folded his test in half and ripped it up into tiny pieces. He stood up and tossed it in the trash.

"Ok, please pass your tests forward." Miss. Abola told the students. Bookie looked around like he was lost. Miss Abola came to his row to collect the papers. Once she got the stack she counted to make sure it was the correct amount.

"Um...Mr. Wentworth...where's your test?" Miss Abola questioned waiting for an explanation.

"I um... threw it out..."

Miss Abola's eyebrows rose. "Well that's just too bad, guess that means it's gonna be a zero then." She walked away from his row to her desk and set down the stack of papers. Bookie couldn't believe his grade could drop from a D- to an F to nothing at all in the same class period.

"Oh come on now Miss Abola. You know I'm your favorite student. You didn't tell me that you were gonna collect it anyway and besides you already know what my grade was."

"You're absolutely right Bookie; I do know what your grade is. It's a zero." Bookie's mouth was wide open in disbelieve.

"I guess I should have just let you fuck me then."

"Go to the office." Miss Abola pointed towards the door.

Bookie was already walking out before she could barely finish.

"Today you have a project due." Mr. Haiter announced to the class.

"I hope you all prepared because it's worth a lot of points." A girl seated in the back named Lisa raised her hand. Mr. Haiter saw her and took a dramatic long sigh.

"What do you want Lisa?"

"How many points is it worth?" Mr. Haiter's eyes darted around the room thinking he already answered that question.

He responded, "A lot."

Lisa's eyes became slanted. "But Mr. Hai-

"Now class, on with the lesson."

Lisa normally wouldn't talk back, but she didn't like being cut off when she had something to say.

"Whatever...MR. HAITER." Lisa bellowed for everyone in class to hear her. Some people smiled and giggled. Mr. Haiter stopped writing on the chalkboard and turned to face Lisa. Everyone's faces quickly went from giggly to serious.

"You know what Lisa; I don't feel like putting up with your damn attitude. So you know what, you can have an attitude for no reason in the office." Mr. Haiter pulled out a detention slip from the teacher's desk. Lisa began flipping her hair with her eyes slightly rolling. She got up from her seat and walked over to Mr. Haiter's desk waiting for the slip. Mr. Haiter handed it to her and Lisa snatched it out of his hand and stormed out of the room.

"And don't come back in here until you learn to shut up." Mr. Haiter yelled after her.

'Someone to stay'

Vancouver sleep clinic

"**M**om where are you? I've been waiting for almost half an hour." Sophie yelled into the speaker of her cell phone. Her mother was supposed to pick her up after school but she never showed up.

"Look Sophie stop yelling and screaming, I'll get there when I get there. Alright?" Her mother reassured her.

"Brenda, I don't live that far away from the school what could possibly be taking you so long?" Sophie was beginning to get restless. She heard Brenda sigh with frustration.

"Sophie just be patient ok?" Sophie heard faint arcade sounding noises.

"Where are you anyway? What's all that noise?" Sophie heard her mother hang the phone up. She took the cell phone away from her ear and stared at it in disbelief.

That bitch just hung up on me. Ok you know what…whatever. I'm just gonna have to take the late bus I guess. She was gathering up her belongings from the bench when she heard the door open and looked to see who it was. Slyder Thomas, still looking as gorgeous as ever, walked out looking and doing something on his phone. He had some car keys in his hand but he didn't seem to notice Sophie standing there.

"Hi." Sophie began. Slyder looked up from his phone and smiled at her. Sophie wanted to know what he thought of her. He was always so genuine and caring to her. And Sophie couldn't have asked for anything better.

"Hey." He came up to her. Sophie gave a shy smile and looked down at the sidewalk.

"How are you?" Slyder said wanting to disrupt the silence.

"I'm alright I guess. How bout you?"

"I'm ok." He smiled once more. And Sophie looked away again. Although she rarely ever looked him in the eyes, she could feel the chemistry they shared. But neither one of them seemed to want to acknowledge it. He slipped his phone back in his jeans pocket.

"Are you waiting for someone to pick you up?" Slyder was taking control of the conversation.

"Yeah I was…until my mom never showed up. I called her but I don't know where she is."

"Well…if it's ok with you I could give you a ride if you want." Sophie's heart stopped beating. Her addiction was getting to her, but she didn't care, that's what she wanted. Her fix was consuming her more and more everyday. But she craved more of it.

"Sure." They began to walk together to the school parking lot and Slyder took his car keys out. Sophie was wondering what kind of car he had, just thinking about it made her palms sweaty. But his car wasn't at all anything she pictured because his car was a baby blue Chevy SS.

Whoa, pretty bad ass car. The closer she got to it the more and more everything around her was dream. By now Sophie was glad her mother didn't pick her up. She liked to think of it as a favoring fate that always arrived at the right time. Slyder opened up the passenger car door for Sophie and she slid down into the tan leather seating. Slyder closed the door and hopped in the driver's side. Slyder was unlike any other guy Sophie had met. He writes poetry, he's not into himself, has a very nice looking car, and he treats her with respect.

They took off down the road and Sophie's stomach decided now would be a great time to demonstrate a loud roar like it was the king of the jungle. Slyder looked over at her and smiled. He pulled into a near by dive on the side of the road. They both walked into the dive, that smelled like grease. Slyder stood there looking at the menu above him, he turned to Sophie.

"So, what do you want?" He simply asked. Sophie walked up to the counter and ordered a hot dog and a fry. She avoided ordering too much food because she didn't want to look like a pig in front of him. When the girl behind the counter told her the cost, Sophie began digging around in her pockets for some loose change and dollars but couldn't seem to come across any. Slyder laid a hand on her arm to stop it from moving.

"Don't worry I got it." He assured her getting out his wallet and handing over the cash. The girl turned around to grab a brown paper bag from the food counter and passed it over to Sophie.

"There you go. Enjoy." She told her giving her a friendly smile. Sophie took a seat in the far corner booth.

"Thanks for paying." Sophie thanked taking a bite out of her hotdog.

"It's no problem." Slyder said calmly.

"You want one?" Sophie offered him a fry.

"No thanks. I'm fine." Slyder answered her. Sophie placed the bag back where it was and continued eating her hotdog and after she was done they walked out to the sun set that shined bright on the skyline coloring the clouds in a pinkish hue. It reminded Sophie of a screen saver on a cell phone. They both got in the car and Slyder continued driving down the road. But not even a few miles down, he stopped again this time near a broken down wooden fence. Slyder got out and Sophie did the same following him over to the fence. He stopped walking and placed his hand on a loose plank. He turned slightly to face Sophie grabbing her hand tightly and she felt an electrifying pulse run through from her hand down her spine. He pushed the plank open and stepped into a junk yard. It had old run down cars, computers, and old cell phones. There were broken beer bottles laying in the grass and pieces of sharp glass. In the far distance Sophie saw an old pale blue run down house that was falling apart.

"What is this place?" Sophie asked Slyder who was leading her through piles of trash and ruined furniture.

"It's called the Knolls." Sophie got a confused look on her face.

"Why is it called the Knolls?" She questioned him still walking through trash.

"Well four years ago, there was this old man who lived in that run down house over there," Slyder pointed to the house he was speaking of in the distance. "His name was John Knolls. And where all this trash is, this used to be his yard. But then he died mysteriously, no one knows how though. So then they decided to turn it into a junk yard since no one was using it or wanted to buy the property. They built this fence around it so no one could get in, but they forgot to repair that loose plank. And ever since then it's just been this way and people sneak in here to hang out and what not." Slyder led her to this blue mustang that had a hole in the roof. He let go of Sophie's hand and climbed on the back of the car and slid down in the gaping hole. He helped Sophie in and she grabbed onto him for support. They sat in the car next to each other.

"Do you come here all the time?" Sophie asked him.

"Yeah mostly, I like it here." Sophie sat up in the seat on her elbows.

"You do?"

Slyder smiled. He gently took her hand.

"Yeah it's peaceful…and quiet." Slyder laced fingers with her, his fingers fit perfectly in the spaces between hers.

"Do you come by yourself?" Sophie asked moving over to him.

"Yeah." Slyder tugged her in closer until Sophie felt his heartbeat against her chest. The bone, muscle, and all grinding against the buttons of her top feeling his rock hard abs. He held her tight wanting to fulfill his need, and her desire. She wanted him to drive her past oblivion, to where he wanted her the most. But from his grasp, she could feel that he would be able to take her beyond what she'd expect.

"It must get lonely here sometimes."

Slyder shook his head.

He felt and stroked her long brunette hair pushing strands from in front of her face ever so gently.

"No…not anymore."

Sophie smiled.

It began to get dark and Slyder was driving Sophie home. She didn't notice it before, but saw writing inside his car. It felt like she was inside a story book. Someone on the outside was looking in, and reading everything about her. Everywhere she looked, there was writing surrounding her. She wondered why she hadn't seen it before. It wasn't in English, it was written in French.

"Did you write all of this in your car?" Sophie asked him still looking at the writing.

He simply nodded his head to respond.

"Oh…so you speak French?"

"Yeah." Slyder smiled at her.

"But then…why are you taking a French class?" She investigated more.

Slyder shrugged concentrated on the shadowy road.

"I guess because it's an easy A."

Sophie pointed to a random sentence that was embedded on the dash board.

"Ok what's that say?"

"Ate pizza with my friend Benny." Sophie pointed to another one on the car door.

"What about that?" Slyder looked over to where she pointed.

"Went skiing with my family." Sophie looked around some more for other written things to ask about. She looked above her and pointed to something.

"What's that say?" Slyder looked to see what she was pointing to.

"Which one?" He asked her.

"Hm…that one." Sophie told him. Slyder stopped in front of Sophie's house turning off the engine. He turned to face Sophie, penetrating her with those eyes so blue, so deep and so true. No matter how much Sophie wanted to look away to escape the trance she was under, she didn't and that's what he wanted. Even though Sophie had a mind, soul, and body of her own, he was in control. It seemed that Slyder enjoyed knowing that, he was avoiding the inevitable for as long as possible. Sophie would soon be his to claim.

"It means I love you…Sophie." Slyder answered her question. He looked away and studied the lonely dark road ahead of them. It became quiet in the car, and Sophie was at a loss of words. The spoken words that left Slyder's lips seemed so promising to her. Sophie got out of the car and walked up to her door step. She didn't even bother saying goodbye or goodnight. She knew that he wasn't saying those exact words to her. But the fact that he said it at all caused her heart to sink. Slyder waited till she was safe in the comfort of her home before driving off.

Meanwhile, Ginger's mother drove her over to the party.

"Thanks mom, I'll see you when I get back." Ginger jumped out of the car and hurried to the front door. She could hear music blasting from behind the glass. Ginger was about to knock placing her hand on the door when she realized that the door was unlocked. Ginger walked into a steaming, hot, and crowded house. Music was booming from the living room to her right, but she was wondering where Bookie was. Then she heard his name being shouted over and over again cheering him on. She followed the loud cheers which lead into the kitchen area. It seemed even hotter in there. Ginger saw Bookie and seven other guys holding a plank that had eight shot glasses glued down all in one line

"Come on! Walk the plank!" A guy from the far back corner yelled. All eight guys picked up the plank and drank their shots. Everyone that crowded around them cheered. Ginger hurried over to him pushing through crowds of people.

"Hey." Ginger said to him. Bookie turned to look at her and he smiled. He pulled her close to him so that their bodies were touching one another.

"Hey cuteness, wanna drink?" He offered playing with her hair. Ginger giggled.

"Sure."

"Alright I'll be right back." Bookie left the kitchen area to go find his friend, Matt. He found him surrounded by girls who were intoxicated sitting on his lap. Bookie pushed the girls aside.

"Hey man she's here it's time to make that drink." Bookie demanded. Matt nodded his head and they both walked to the bathroom hidden in the dark corner of the house. Matt took a glass he had placed there earlier from off of the sink. He grabbed a bottle of vodka from under the sink cabinet. Matt opened the bottle and poured more than half into the glass. He took out a pouch of powder from his jeans pocket and emptied it into the glass. Bookie watched as the powder turned into dust, and then dissolved into the vodka.

Bookie immediately grabbed the glass and left the bathroom. He hurriedly pushed through drunken crowds over to the kitchen area where Ginger was waiting.

"Here you go. Drink up." Bookie handed Ginger the glass. She took a sip, while Bookie was making himself a drink.

"A toast." He held up his glass and Ginger held up hers. The glasses clanked together and they both chugged down their drink. Bookie knew that the good time he was waiting for was about to happen after making her a few more glasses for her. After a while, like expected, Ginger became disoriented. Bookie smiled and grabbed her around her waist. He kissed her gently.

"You wanna go upstairs and talk for a little bit?" Bookie offered. Ginger gave a drunken smile. But Bookie was already leading her to the stairs before she could give an answer. Ginger sluggishly walked with Bookie behind her, his arms around her torso. Once they reached the staircase he hulled her over his broad shoulder and carried her upstairs. Bookie could hear Ginger mumbling and groaning as he carried her down the hallway to a bedroom. He eased her down until both her feet were placed on the rug. Ginger giggled, her eyes slightly closed.

"Bookie where are we goin?" Ginger asked him. Bookie smiled opening the bedroom door.

"Shh." He told her. Bookie peeked inside of the room to make sure no one was in there. Luckily for him the room was empty, waiting for him. Bookie took Ginger's hand pulling her into the room with him. And Ginger, like a puppet on a string, followed him with the same drunken smile. Bookie laid her on the bed, and closed the door.

'Summer Breeze'

Seals and Crofts

OMG!!! The only day that I get time to myself, my annoying, socially damaging cousin, Marribell, is coming to visit. OOKKK...I gotta prepare myself,

1) No malls
2) No parks
3) No theaters
4) No downtown gathering spots
5) No meeting friends

Ok I think that covers it.

"Greetings Sophie", Marribell said putting her hand up, open palm, next to her face.

And it begins, Sophie thought, *better play along*.

"Howdy", Sophie retorted, trying to sound and appear enthused by Marribell's awkward appearance. Marribell was wearing red, black, & yellow skinny jeans with an argyle vest, and converse shoes. *Hello and goodbye to my social life...and reputation.*

"So I'm thinking we should go to this new restaurant called Bossie", Marribell said gathering her red shag scarf and pink pock-a-dot coat.

"O..o..o..k..k..k.." Sophie said hesitating, remembering her list of things to prevent social disaster. "Where is it Marribell?"

"It's new…It's a new restaurant!"

"Ummmm…you said that already…"

"Let's go" Marribell grabbed Sophie by her wrist and ran out the door.

In the car Marribell secured her annoying reputation by humming "Summer Breeze"…the whole 30 min ride to the "new restaurant".

SHIT!!!! Sophie exclaimed, realizing Marribell had parked her car in the lot of the most popular mall, in the most popular town, at the most popular time of day. *Of course this would fuckin happen to me…ok..ok think. How do ditch the problem.*

"Sophie?!?!", Marribell whined, waiting for her to catch up, "come on, I tried to make reservations for 1:00. Let's giddy up!" Sophie watched as her disaster date skipped to the main entrance of the mall. Sophie was paralyzed from shock. Her social life was tapping her on the shoulder saying *"Are you sure you wanna do this? Just pretend to be sick. Say you forgot you had a dentist appointment. Say you have the measles or…or…or Syphilis."*

Yeah Syphilis….that'll work, Sophie thought.

"Sophie! We can't wait until the jibbers are jabbin" Marribell yelled from the entrance.

"Maybe not!" Sophie realized as she forced herself to comply.

"Oh…while we're here, I need to go get some new socks."

Let me guess, argyle right? To match that hideous vest. Marribell strolled over to the shelf of socks.

"Hmmmm…well…let's see…I can get purple, pink, or blue. But hm…I don't think those would match."

Is she serious?? Did she just say those wouldn't match? She looks like a cross between the Mad Hatter, and Peewee Herman, I don't think anything in this store would match.

Marribell turns to Sophie, who was standing there covering her face up with one hand peeking through her fingers to avoid seeing anyone she'd know.

"What do you think Soph, should I get purple, pink or blue socks?" Sophie's face was blank for a second. *Wow, she is serious.*

"Um…I don't think it really matters. Get what you like." Knowing in the back of her mind that whatever Marribell would pick, it would just blend in with all the other mess she had on her back. Marribell continued scanning the shelf when she noticed a pair of argyle socks hidden in the back.

"OOOOO!!" Marribell screeched excited to find some socks that she liked. Without delay she snatched them off the shelf. Sophie didn't think Marribell could look any more foolish than she already did.

Damn this store to hell! Sophie screamed in her head. But once she laid her eyes on the argyle socks that were probably hidden for a reason, she knew that her reputation had hit rock, hard, solid bottom. Sophie couldn't help but let out a loud gasp of utter disgust. Marribell turned to her.

"What?"

"Nothing." Sophie quickly responded, straightening out her face. Marribell turned her attention back to the argyle socks.

"I'm...."

Please don't get them. Please don't say you're getting them anything but those.

"Gettin' 'em."

Damn it! Marribell skipped to the counter, and in the process cut some people off who were about to pay for their things. Sophie made sure to wait a long distance away, pretending that she didn't know her. She looked at the clock, and it was now 1:29.

"I'm gonna go to the bathroom and see if they fit." Marribell waltzed into the womens' bathroom, leaving Sophie sitting there waiting.

To see if they fit? What the hell? She waits, and waits and waits.

Maybe they didn't fit. Sophie glances at the clock once more; it was now 1:42. *Well...looks like we missed our reservations.* Marribell finally resurfaced.

"Well, I tried 'em on." She walked toward her.

Sophie's eyes slanted, replied, "O...o...k...k."

"Well, let's get movin' noodle." Marribell walked with Sophie following behind. A couple people walking passed shot Marribell interesting looks, like she was an endangered species of geek.

Maybe I can write this excursion off as charity on my taxes. Sophie realized.

"Um…what made you wear that outfit?" Sophie asked trying to make the question appear as non-judgmental as possible. Marribell paused and giggled a bit.

"I couldn't be naked." Marribell laughed hysterically. Sophie's eyes were slanted again.

"O…o…k…k, but um…what made you decide to wear THAT."

"Well you know, my policy is, I like to wear all of my favorite things at once."

What the fuck? "Well where are the socks?"

Marribell giggled once more.

"I'm wearin 'em."

Sophie looked down at Marribell's feet thinking that no one would be able to see them since she has on skinny jeans. But because Sophie's the luckiest person alive, they're tube socks. Marribell now looked like an oversized Oompa Loompa. Her jeans were rolled up to her knees, and the socks were pulled up just below them.

How the hell can you roll up skinny jeans?

"Oh you like them? I know they're cute, that must be why you're so speechless and in shock." Marribell stated posing in her outfit. Glancing at the clock, Marribell shrieked, "Oh whoppers, we better get going before we miss our reservations." She continued walking with Sophie.

"Um…we already missed it, didn't you make reservations for 1:00?" Sophie asked her.

"Well I tried to make reservations but they wouldn't let me."

"Then…why did we rush…?"

"Oh because I had to get some socks." Marribell answered her.

"Um…o…o…k…k."

Marribell was too busy walking, looking at her new socks that she bumped into someone. "Oh jeepers I'm sorry about that." Marribell apologized. Sophie looked at the guy they bumped into.

He is fucking hot. Oh my gosh, his hair. Oh and those sunset hazel eyes they could talk you into doing anything.

"Marribell?" The guy asked.

Oh my gosh…if this guy knows her, I swear I'm gonna swallow some bleach tonight, with a shot of anti-freeze for flavor.

"Yeah, that's me. What are you doing here Phil?" Phil smiled, placing his hands in his pockets, looking shockingly nervous to talk to her.

"The Jasmines are in bloom." Phil reminisced.

"Yeah the Jasmines, I remember we planted them last year. Yeah yeah yeah." Marribell whined.

You've got to be kidding me. Sophie thought.

"I missed coming home from a hard days work and you're waitin' there, not a care in the world." Phil said desperately.

"Well… late for reservations." Marribell disregarded.

"Who's your friend?" Phil gestured towards Sophie.

"Oh she's not my friend, she's my cousin." Marribell informed him.

Shit, shit, shit, shit.

Phil glanced around for a second in silence.

"Oh ok…I see…um…well anyway I gotta go." He said walking away.

"Oh and uh, I've always loved that outfit on you. But the socks are new." Phil gave a wink before disappearing down the escalator. Marribell smiled.

"Yeah that was just Phil he's my ex boyfriend. His dad owns a bank; he's still totally in love with me."

What?... That was her ex boyfriend?... Here's this guy who looks like he could be an Abercrombie model, and he went out with that? They don't even look good together. He's gotta be deaf, dumb and stupid… Definitely adding arsenic to my cocktail tonight.

Sophie and Marribell managed their way to the "new restaurant." She dared to think Bossie was just a small café place that had just opened with hardly any customers. But of course it wasn't small, and it wasn't a café.

I'm so screwed. Doesn't this place have a dress code? I mean how is Marribell getting in?

"Are you ladies ready to order or…" The waiter asked.

"No I'm ready to go; I'm just waiting on this little peacock."

Yeah…that was cool.

"Ok, well what would you like to drink miss?" The waiter asked Marribell.

"Hm…can I just get an ice tea please? And what do you want Soph?"

"I'll just get the lemonade I guess."

"You know, I think I'm gonna go to the bathroom real quick. Would you please sit here and watch Joe?"

"Who?" Sophie said confused.

"Joe." Marribell removed her bag strap from around her shoulder, placing it on the table. Joe sported a bedazzled name tag with matching rhinestone winking face.

What did I ever do to deserve this humiliation?? Was it because I failed my test and lied to my mom about it? Because I just have a dumb ass cousin?? Like what is it? Sophie was mesmerized by Joe. He was so "dazzling"; then she realized, *this damn bag is fucking mocking me. It's looking at me and saying, "Gotcha!!!"*

Breaking her trance, Sophie found Marribell walking backwards, holding a conversation. She backed into an occupied table, knocking over glasses.

"Hey weezer I'm back. What did I miss?"

"Phil." Sophie answered her.

"You know…I keep thinking I forgot something." Marribell said ignoring her.

"To match." Sophie mumbled.

"What was that?" Marribell asked her.

Marribell managed to restrain herself from creating a natural disaster when the waiter brought the food out.

"I didn't say anything." Sophie lied slicing her lobster tail.

"Oh my fruit loops this thing is so tough I can't even cut it."

Well no the fuck duh Marribell you cant cut it, it's very very well done.

Marribell stood up in her seat and used all her might to cut the steak, giving off cavemen grunts in the process.

Sophie slammed her fork and knife down, shot up meeting Marribell in her eyes.

"Shut up!!!…Shut the fuck up!!!…You've been ridiculous, fucking ridiculous all day long. You are on my last reserved nerve. Between the outfit, the socks, and your ridiculously gorgeous ex boyfriend, I can't stand another moment…another second. You are sucking my life and my reputation with each fucking move you make! Shit!"

"Well…" Marribell said matter-of-factly, "I know what this is about."

"Well?" Sophie questioned with raised eyebrows, anticipating another boneheaded remark.

"This is about Slyder." Marribell retorted, seeming worried.

"What?…"

"You should stay away from him, he has a past." Marribell warned. Sophie was taken aback by Marribell's shift in mood. "I'm serious. Just promise me."

'Oh'

Okay

'He has a past.' Was all that was running through Sophie's mind the next day in French class. But whenever she turned around to face Slyder, he looked harmless what could he possibly have done that would make Marribell of all people even be cautious of him. Slyder always waited by her locker for her in the mornings, after school, and after French class. Whenever they'd hang out and go to a restaurant he would never hesitate to pay. Slyder was always the perfect gentleman around her and she'd hate to end their companionship just because some crazy cousin of hers advised her to. The classical music began to ring aloud and everyone in the class turned in their quizzes. Sophie met Slyder outside of the classroom walking with him to his locker.

"So how'd you like the quiz?" Slyder asked.

Sophie shrugged. "I didn't really get a chance to study, I think I failed it."

Slyder smiled.

"But of course it was easy for you right?" Sophie laughed.

Slyder smiled closing his locker lacing his fingers with hers walking down the hall.

"Just don't tell Ms. Pompe that." Slyder joked.

Later on that day, Sophie was in Ginger's room while Ginger was uploading some photos on Pixel Me. Ginger took a look at all the photos going through them with Sophie. But after a while Sophie noticed Ginger with a guy she didn't recognize in most of the pictures.

"Who's he?" Sophie wondered.

Ginger giggled. "Oh that's Drew, he's my boyfriend now." Ginger clicked through more and more pictures of them either kissing or hugging or holding hands in the park.

"Oh since when?" Sophie asked.

"Since like…a couple days ago."

"But…I thought you said I was going to meet him first before you said anything…"

"Well…I was going to invite you the night we took these pictures but…he just wanted it to be the two of us. So, I just didn't."

Sophie nodded her head awkwardly looking down at the floor.

"So." Ginger nudged Sophie smiling. "I saw you and Slyder today holding hands."

Sophie laughed and blushed a little. "Yeah, but we're not…you know dating or anything. But I really think we're on our way there though."

"But you guys looked so adorable together." Ginger smiled.

All Sophie did was smile some more. "Yeah, it feels weird though, because I can't believe this is actually happening."

"What?"

"Well, just being with Slyder like that, and him holding my hand and everything."

Ginger was about to say something when her phone alarmed her about a text message. "Hold on a second." She said responding to the text and then she placed her phone down on her computer desk. "Ok sorry about that. So you really think there's something there?"

Sophie smiled. "Yeah I really do and-

Ginger's phone went off again. "Sorry." She said responding to the text smiling and giggling. She placed the phone face up on the desk once again. "Ok you were saying?"

"I was saying that, yeah I really do think there's something special between us. And Ginger he's so nice and-

The same obnoxious annoying text ring tone of a train's whistle went off interrupting Sophie again. But before Ginger could snatch it up Sophie got a good look at who was texting her. She thought it would be Drew but surprisingly she saw the initials ST.

ST? Who in the world could ST be? Hm whatever.

Ginger kept texting on her phone this time longer than Sophie was willing to wait around for.

"You know…I think I'm just gonna go. I'll see you." Sophie got up from the spinning office chair grabbing her purse off of Ginger's bed.

"Hey wait," Ginger began before Sophie could walk out. "Are you coming to my recital this weekend?"

Sophie turned to face her. "Um, I don't know." She didn't say anything more and she didn't care to. She just left, a little irritated that she didn't bother contacting her to meet Drew. *Like I said only a matter of time.* Once she got home, she decided she'd log onto her Pixel Me account to customize her profile a little bit. She saw statuses and posts from people she's befriended. Sophie noticed Ginger posted a status a few seconds ago that said: Time to go have some real fun with my love Drew <3 ☺

Sophie just rolled her eyes and logged off.

My love? Are you kidding me? It's barely even been 48 hours and already he's your love? It wasn't the fact that Ginger had a boyfriend that annoyed her the most. It was the way Ginger was treating her as a friend now that she had one. Sophie should've seen this coming more than a mile away. But she's known Ginger since the kindergarten, and ever since it wasn't a problem in school to actually like guys and get over the cooty stage, Ginger has had boyfriend after boyfriend since day one. All the guys liked her, all the guys wanted her, and all the guys loved her. It would never be her, it would always be Ginger.

"Alright class please put your books away. We're going to watch a movie about the Civil War. And I know you guys are excited about that, aren't you?" The teacher said with enthusiasm over all the groans from the students loading the disc into the computer. A few people put their heads down and others took out their phone to text. Sophie put her head down on her notebook trying her best to pay attention to watch the movie. She heard a faint giggle behind her and observed Ginger secretly reading a note. Ginger took her pencil scribbling something down and folded it back eyeing the teacher closely making sure he didn't see her. Ginger ducked her head down and tossed the note and Sophie watched as the square piece of paper landed in the hands of Slyder Thomas. At first Sophie was in a complete state of shock and thought her eyes were playing tricks on her. She looked back at Ginger who kept staring at him smiling.

What the fuck is she smiling about? And why the hell are they even talking to each other? Sophie took out her pencil and scribbled down on her notebook: What the hell are you doing?

She immediately tore out the piece of paper not caring if the teacher heard her. Sophie crumpled it up into a ball and through it at Ginger letting it hit her arm. Ginger turned to face her and opened up the crumpled ball but before it looked like she could even think of a response Slyder tossed his note back to her. Ginger just disregarded Sophie's note and responded to Slyder's instead.

What....the....fuck? Sophie turned around and tried to pay attention to the movie again, but all she could really hear were the tossing of paper and giggling and laughing. She wished that the bell of Symphony number 5 would come on ending this period so she could go to study hall in the nice quiet library and calm down. After trying her best to watch the boring movie for what seemed like hours her symphony came on and Sophie was the first one out of the class. And usually this period Slyder and her would be walking together but she didn't bother waiting up for him. She made her way to the library walking into the soothing playing of the violins and the harp. Sophie took a seat at a round table by herself gathering out her books still thinking about what she had seen. A butler came by with a tray of mints on a silver platter offering her some but she didn't want any. She was too occupied with seeing Ginger and Slyder walking into the library together and taking a seat next to each other a few tables away.

What the fuck is going on? Like did I die or something? Am I ghost??? Is this a dream? Is she serious???? Sophie sat there in disbelieve, staring at them flipping through a book together smiling and laughing. Her own best friend stabbed her in the back and it hurt. Sophie didn't believe that they were both that blind; they had to have seen her sitting there. Neither one of them even took it upon themselves to invite her to their table they left her out there stranded on an Island with a butler holding a plate of mints, but at least he was considerate even if he was getting paid. *If I could murder her and get away with it she would've been dead by now.* And Sophie was left sitting there, watching them flirt and giggle enjoying each other's company surrounded by the playing of violins and the harp. Like she thought, it would never be Sophie, it would always be Ginger.

'Move On'

Anna Von Hausswolff

Her phone began vibrating against her night table waking Sophie from her nice nap. She looked and saw Ginger texted her reminding her about her recital if she was still going. Sophie was thinking about not showing up still trying to get over how bogus she's been to her lately. Sophie didn't respond and just laid back down in the comfort of her bed wanting to sleep all her pain away. Sophie sat up and texted Slyder asking him if he wanted to hang out somewhere today. Not even a few moments later he responded telling her he might have to work today and he'd probably be busy after. Sophie could hear her parents downstairs arguing about something which was probably nothing important.

"Can't you just do this one thing for me Terrance?" Brenda asked slamming the dishes into the dish washer.

"But Brenda you already know its time for my evening nap."

"But I have…something to do." Brenda said awkwardly turning away from him, trying to ignore the sudden silence.

"Oh really…and where do you have to go?" Terrance questioned moving into the kitchen from the living room.

"I…have some errands to run and…I figured that you know you could take Sophie to Ginger's recital tonight. I'm sure she wouldn't wanna miss it."

"Yeah fuck that recital." Sophie whispered to herself from on the top of the stairs.

"Look, if she wants to go I'll take her. But what I wanna know is where you're gonna be."

Brenda took a sigh brushing back some loose blonde strands back into her tight bun. "Well I was gonna run some quick errands and then…spend the rest of the night with some girlfriends that's all. Oh, hey and by the way, do you have some money I could borrow and I'll pay you back?"

Terrance's eye brows wrinkled. "Why do you need money for?"

"I just needed some to have in my pocket incase I have an emergency that's all."

"How much do you need?" Terrance got his wallet out.

"Like…40 dollars if that's possible."

Terrance looked at her in disbelief at first, but then just handed the money over.

"Thank you. I'll pay you back when I can." Brenda stuffed the money inside her pocket.

Then they both heard Sophie come downstairs and Brenda continued washing dishes and Terrance went back into the living room.

"You know Brenda I've decided I wasn't gonna go to Ginger's recital."

Brenda turned around causing soap bubbles and water to splash on the floor. "What why?"

Sophie shrugged. "I just don't wanna go. I'm tired and I'd rather stay here and take a nap."

"But honey, wouldn't you rather go see your best friend? I mean I'm sure she'd like it if you went. You should go. Remember in 4th grade when she came to see the play that you were in? She was so excited."

"Yeah but the only two parts I had was a bush, and then a messenger who only had one line. And then for the rest of the play I was a bush."

Brenda took off her yellow rubber gloves throwing them on the sink.

"Honey, just go. Ok? I promise you'll love it and when it's over you can tell me all about it when you get back." Brenda assured her directing her upstairs. Sophie went back into her room and she got dressed anyway. Even though she really didn't want to go because she hated Ginger more than anything at that moment, but her mother insisted on her going. Later once Sophie arrived at the dance hall, she texted Ginger and told her she was here. She waited by the door watching crowds of people going into the auditorium taking their seats. Sophie saw Ginger rushing up to her from down the hall. Her face was glittery and perfectly polished. Her lips were scarlet red with her brown hair pulled back into a high bun. Ginger gave Sophie a hug, ever since they were little no matter how bogus Ginger was to Sophie, Ginger was always happy to see her.

"I'm so glad you came. How do I look?" Ginger asked looking in the body length mirror making sure her tutu fit her curves perfectly.

Sophie nodded. "You look great."

Ginger ran both of her hands across her hair making sure no strands were left hanging letting out a sigh of relief. "Good, I wanted to look fantastic for this performance. You should go get a seat I'm about to take place back stage. Wish me luck." Ginger said once more giving her another warm embrace then rushing away leaving a sweet lingering smell of perfume. Sophie went into the auditorium the lights still bright and she made her way over to an empty seat the lights became to dim until it was completely dark. Sophie sat down in the second row in the seat closest to the aisle. She wished Slyder would have came with; she could have used some of his company. The audience began to applaud as the ballet teacher came onto the stage. She waved at everyone giving a huge grin and cleared her throat before speaking. "Ladies and gentlemen boys and girls welcome to our ballet recital called Pedal of a Rose. I am Miss. Chompit, and the performance you are about to see today was actually directed by one of our other coaches here in the hall but unfortunately they were unable to make it. The people you will see performing today worked very very hard and I am proud of all of them let's give them a hand." The audience applauded once more.

"Now without futher ado, please make sure your cell phones are on silent or completely off during the performance. If it's an emergency then please step outside into the hall as you would not like to disturb the performers. And thank you all for coming enjoy the performance."

The teacher quickly walked off stage behind the grand sapphire curtain. Sophie jumped at the sudden sound of a grand piano begin to play and out came a group of ballet dancers spinning and leaping across the stage. Sophie tried to see if she could see Ginger anywhere in the group but she didn't.

Sophie continued to watch the performance of the graceful ballet dancers in tune with the music with every leap, spin, and lift. The group ended their performance a little while later by leaping one by one in a line away behind the curtains while violins played softly in the background. The next performance was a solo, and Sophie recognized the girl that came onto the stage. She was the tall dark skinned girl, Somone, who Ginger didn't like. Somone began on one side of the stage and when the music began pointed her toe high in the air and began to spin across the stage effortless letting the soft classical music carry her every move.

Meanwhile, Brenda, hopped into the car after running her quick errands and meeting her girlfriends up for some dinner, called her bank to check her bank account. She sat in the parking lot in front of the restaurant on her cell phone and the monotoned woman's voice informed her she had 35 dollars and 32 cents. Brenda immediately hung up the phone throwing it down on the floor in between her feet under the gas and the break pedals.

"Shit!" She yelled in frustration hitting the steering wheel. She was really planning on going to the casino today but she couldn't go anymore with that much money in the bank. Plus, she realized that she needed to pay Sophie's tuition for school at the end of this year. She spent most of the money that Sophie's grandmother left her in her will from being a woman's rights activist and being the head leader of the first founded school for women of all color who wanted to get an education.

"Shit shit shit!" Brenda yelled once more hitting the steering wheel. But she thought about it and figured that she'd just go to the casino this one time. And she couldn't loose this time, she just couldn't. She put on her seat belt speeding off down the road towards downtown.

Later, at the dance hall, after plenty of good performances Ginger's was the last one to go with her ballet partner. The performance began with them starting at opposite ends of the stage and once the music started Ginger ran lightly over to her partner and caressed him and he did the same. Then he lifted her in the air spinning her around while Ginger was in a stilled pose with her arms straight out as she descended down to the ground. Sophie typically didn't like ballet but these performances she's seen so far have been pretty good and not all that bad. Ginger began to leap over and over to the edge of the stage looking out straight at the blinding spot light that was making her sparkle and twinkle like the sun shine over the ocean. Her partner lifted her up in the air, his strong biceps flexing as he carried her around until they were in each other's arms in the middle of the stage. Ginger looked up at him and she turned away leaping to the edge of the curtain away from him leaving him on stage until he leaped away in the opposite direction behind the curtain. Right away, the audience stood up cheering and whistling loudly. Sophie stood up to clap while at the same time trying to cover her ears from the whistling guy next to her. The full crew came from behind the curtain chained in hands giving a bow at the edge of the stage. Then they all went behind the curtain and the lights came back on in the auditorium and the aisles flooded with people like wildfire. Luckily for Sophie it was easy for her to slip right out since she sat in the chair closest to the aisle. Sophie went out in the hall back where Ginger greeted her and right away Ginger came rushing out panting out of breath.

"Did you see me? Was I good?" Ginger asked excitedly between taking deep breaths.

"Yeah you were amazing, I really liked it. It was great." Sophie complimented her giving her a hug.

Ginger smiled and giggled. "Thanks, I was sooo nervous I was shaking like crazy." Her phone alerted her of a text message and she quickly grabbed it out of her satchel purse. Sophie was standing next to her over her shoulder and saw the initials ST again. She watched Ginger type: Was I good? How did you like it?

ST responded right away saying: I loved it, you looked great. The performance was beautiful.

Ginger responded: Thanks, but I'm gonna have to give up dancing soon but at least I got to do this performance before I have to quit.

Where are you?

ST responded: I'm looking for you, where are you?

Ginger was about to text back, but stopped and Sophie noticed her waving at someone in the crowd of people coming out of the auditorium. And Sophie tried to see, and once she noticed who it was she wished she was never Ginger's friend, and she wished she never came. Slyder Thomas was seen waving at her making his way through the crowd over to her. Sophie looked at him with betrayed eyes, then back at Ginger and both of them seemed to have little interest in acknowledging her presence. Before Slyder could reach the both of them Sophie let out a sound of disgust slamming through the double doors of the dance hall zipping up her grey hoodie. And this was the last and final straw of their friendship. Suddenly the initials ST all made sense. It stood for Slyder Thomas of course why she hadn't thought about it before she had no clue. Ginger doesn't know how long she spent going through almost everyone she knew, and even people she barely even knew names that would fit the initials ST when all along it was the person who she knew the most, her own friend other than Ginger, Slyder Thomas. Just the thought of how easy it could have been for her to figure it out in front of Ginger that same day she first saw the initials if she just took a step back and thought about it angered her. Sophie was a mixture of emotions. *By now I would have been cussing them out in my head. Damning them all to hell, hating and beating myself up for trusting people like them. I thought I had it all clear, all out in the clear. But there's just some things you don't need to hear.*

'Pale Horses'

Moby

Sophie strongly typed, FUCK EVERYONE. She didn't press enter right away in the status bar wondering if she really meant that. But moving through her mind were all of the moments that made her come to this anger she was feeling, she was pretty sure it was acceptable. She pressed the enter key and a sudden knock caused Sophie to snap out of thought. She turned the screen off of her computer.

"Sophie?" Brenda opened up the bedroom door. "I have... something to tell you." Sophie's stomach was becoming a sink hole. "I called the school...yesterday...and I told them that you were...um... transferring..."

"Transferring? What do you mean?" Sophie questioned. Brenda looked a bit uneasy, straightening out her blouse.

"You're transferring to another school; you're not going back to Vermyear Academy." At first, Sophie found it as a relief about not going back she wouldn't have to see Ginger, and most of all Slyder's face again. But then she found herself thinking about all the people she had met there. And all the memories she had, and now she was leaving just when she began to get comfortable.

"What school am I gonna go to?"

"Cornegey Hall."

Cornegey Hall was a hot topic in the rumor mill and said to be the worst school on the block or even in the whole town for that matter. It was like death row compared to all the other schools in the district, not only because of the teachers, but the students too. Sophie would choose to go anywhere besides there any day.

"You'll be going there tomorrow." Without further discussion Brenda walked out of the room leaving Sophie there speechless. She didn't understand why the sudden transfer. *Well at least I won't have to wear that damn uniform.* She looked at the uniform hanging on her closet neatly ironed. *But even that's better than Cornegey Hall.*

The next day, was the day. The day Sophie had to leave all her friends, all the memories, and the school she would probably never see again.

"I hope you have a good day at school honey, trust me, you'll love it." Brenda grabbed her coat and purse and left. Sophie was sitting in the kitchen looking at the clock, counting down the minutes when she would have to go to her death sentence. She couldn't even get a goodnight sleep without counting down the time she had even then.

Sophie got on the bus with all the other kids. In her mind, she pictured it being a prison bus taking them all to jail. The bus was quiet, and no one was saying a word. Sophie stared out the window at the gloomy day. She was lost at sea. Aimless. The whole ride that was the only thing on her mind. The bus rolled up to the school, and plastered on the brick wall, were supposed to be the words Cornegey Hall, but someone took bright pink chalk and replaced the letter 'a' in hall, which had fallen off the wall, with an e. Sophie knew she wasn't going to have a good experience, and just when things couldn't get any worse for her, when who but Marribell strolls up to Sophie's side.

"Sophie??? You go here? I didn't know that."

"I wish I didn't." Sophie mumbled.

"What was that?" Marribell asked.

"Nothing." Sophie quickly answered. Marribell's outfit looked even worse than when Sophie saw her last time. Instead of red skinny jeans, she had yellow ones. Along with stripped purple socks, a plain beige shirt with a vest covered in pop tabs. And who else did Sophie see but her Joe bag still bedazzled as ever being carried along.

I really don't wanna be here. I just want someone to take me somewhere else, just send me on my own. I just wanna go back to my own home.

Sophie looked down at the ground counting every leaf she stepped over to avoid eye contact with anyone. People were pushing past her, kids running and yelling. Although the school wasn't as crowded as Vermyear Academy, it looked bigger. The school looked trashy and filthy, everywhere papers were flying, pop cans, gum wrappers, and scribbled writings on the walls in chalk. This made Sophie feel intimidated, not to mention her only friend for the time being was her annoying weird cousin Marribell. But Sophie figured she might as well just stick along with her and look like an idiot with Marribell, Sophie had nothing else to loose. She made her way through the crowd nearing the schools outer lockers, a sudden whiff of smoke stroked her face allowing the strong, but sweet smell to pass through her.

Are you fucking kidding me? Great, first it was the sudden dumb ass transfer, then my annoying cousin Marribell, and now there are smokers on campus??

Sophie turned her head to the direction in which the smoke had come from. Standing there in the midst of the thin smoke was a boy, a boy with black hair. He seemed to be so still mixed in with chaos surrounding him. From around the corner appeared a tall woman, long wavy blonde hair. She stared at the boy for a second, and then approached him and she took the cigarette from in between the boy's lips. The woman took a drag of the cigarette and threw it to the ground. Sophie broke away from her glance continuing her walk. Ahead of Sophie was Marribell waiting.

"Geeze mageeze, what were you staring at Sophie?"

"Nothing, I wasn't staring at anything." Sophie walked faster trying to loose Marribell in the crowd. Marribell pushed through everyone to get to Sophie's side.

"So what's your first class?" Sophie didn't want to answer her, because she was afraid that Marribell would have the same.

"What's yours?" Sophie asked her instead, hoping she didn't end up hating herself.

"Oh mine's Chemistry."

Dam! Dam! Dam! Sophie hated this school already.

Everyone in class took their seat, Sophie was miserable in the corner with Marribell sitting next to her. In came the teacher the same woman Sophie had seen outside with the long wavy blonde hair.

"Alright, good morning class. I have a few announcements to make. First thing, don't forget about the science fair if you choose to sign up. And we also have a new student joining our class today, her name is Sophie Gribsie. I want you all to make her feel welcome in class."

Sophie sunk into her seat, shyly taking quick glances at her surroundings. A few friendly people gave a smile, others just stared. Especially a certain someone she had noticed earlier. The boy Sophie had seen smoking outside sat directly across from her, giving him a clear view of her. Sophie tried not to make eye contact, but the more she tried to avoid his stare, the more she'd keep looking at him. He just kept staring at her. Intently, his bright yellowish eyes staring deep into her. This made Sophie uncomfortable. Not only because she didn't even know him, but he didn't even know her.

The teacher's voice slowly became mumbles to Sophie's ears. As far as Sophie was concerned she was in another world, a world where she wasn't the wanting any longer, but the wanted.

"Psst! Are you gonna take the paper you silly lamb?" Marribell whispered, holding in her hand a stack of papers.

"Oh sorry." Sophie's attention turned back to the reality of things.

"Now class," The teacher began, "I want you to write down the answers to these questions on the board ok? And then after that, we are going to discuss it in class alright?"

A few students started to copy down the questions written. Sophie was a little bit sidetracked. From the corner of her eye, she could see the boy sitting across from her writing something on his paper.

"Oh you know what? I don't think we'll probably have time to go over this in class, so when you're done writing it down why don't you just come up here and place it on the desk."

Sophie stood up to join the crowd of students surrounding the teacher's desk. The boy had laid his paper down, on the paper in big black lettering was the word FUCK.

Well he's definitely gonna fail for sure.

"Anyone else still working?" No one answered the teacher's question. The teacher asked to see Sophie after class.

"Hi Sophie I don't think I've really gotten a chance to introduce myself to you, my name is Ms. Hendrick. She gave her a pleasant smile, Sophie did the same. "Do you have any questions for me at all?"

Sophie shook her head no.

"Alright, well come see me if you have any questions, my door is always open." Sophie walked out of class suddenly startled by an annoying voice.

"Hiya! Where were ya?" Marribell shrieked. Sophie rolled her eyes.

"Don't you have somewhere to be?"

"Hmm…not really I have lunch soon like..5th period."

Sophie stopped walking.

"Are you fucking kidding me? You have lunch that period?" Marribell's eyes widened.

"Then I guess that means you do too." Sophie ignored her, turning around the other way nearly missing someone. But when she realized who it was, everything around her was just blank, anything and everything was allowed to make a noise a sound, a cry, anything, but they chose to stay silent. It was the same yellow eyes, the same black hair, the intense vibe, but only this time up close. He brushed passed Sophie.

"Who is that guy?" Sophie whispered to Marribell.

"He's scary isn't he? I mean…he just looks so…full of…anger… and and….and rage… Don't even get me started on those yellow eyes of his."

"I just asked for his name Marribell."

"It's Entino Auwz." It stuck inside her mind, intertwining with her memory. As far as Sophie was concerned, Marribell was wrong about Entino. He wasn't full of anger or rage, but of lust and desire. These thoughts colliding in her head surprised her, it felt like she had known him for a lifetime, and yet knew nothing about him.

Sophie wanted to know why this was happening to her. She wanted to go back to some place gentle and familiar, like Slyder's arms. Sophie despised this school, and everything and anything inside of it. The most puzzling part, the tiniest bit of her soul was telling her to stay, her mind said she hated this school, but her heart was contradicting it.

Sophie placed her tray down on the table, Marribell and her other weird friends sitting with her. To Sophie, she was lost, like she took the wrong way home. Suddenly, one pair of wide bear hands smashed on the table in front of her, breaking Sophie away from her chain of thought.

"Go away Chris." Marribell demanded. Chris ignored her, his dark shadowy eyes staring straight into Sophie's.

"So uh…" Chris began, "You're the new kid I heard."

Sophie nodded, not knowing what else to say. Chris studied her for a moment, grinding his teeth together. Marribell leaned in closer to Sophie.

"I said…go away Chris." His eyes darted in Marribell's direction.

"Hey you shut the fuck up you troll." Marribell sunk in to her seat, putting her head down. Chris turned his attention back to Sophie, still speechless.

"So, you wanna go out with me?" Chris asked giving a wink licking his lips.

"Um, no…?" Sophie spat.

Chris's face straightened and his eyes slanted. A few people at the table smiled and giggled. Chris gave them a stare which made them silence and clear their throats.

"Well then you know what? I'm gonna make your life a living hell. Just wait and see, you're not even gonna make it out alive." Chris stood straight up and looked at everyone at the table.

"None of ya are." He spat on the ground and walked away, He glared back over his shoulder a few times before sitting down. The rest of the period, Chris kept mouthing insults to Marribell and her friends.

"Alright everyone get in your squads." The gym teacher, Ms. Vogess announced. Sophie hated her gym uniform. The shirt was too tight, and the shorts were too short. Sophie wished she had gotten a Large instead of a Medium.

"Ok stay seated, I'll be right back I forgot something in the office." Once Ms. Vogess was out of sight, Sophie heard someone yell,

"Oh hey look, its fat ass!" Sophie turned around, and who else could it be screaming it but Chris. She didn't realize it at first, but all eyes were on her. Students were whispering and laughing with Chris pointing. Students kept egging him on. For the first time in a while in school, Sophie was about to cry. She tried to hold them back, but a few tears ran down her cheek and before she knew it she was crying. Sophie stood up and ran out of the gym. She ran into the locker room grabbed her belongings and rushed to a nearby bathroom. Sophie never felt so embarrassed in her life. She was sobbing trying to change back into street clothes, but she couldn't help but sit on the toilet seat crying. Her first day here and she already had people who hated her. Sophie didn't dare to go back to the gym; she was guaranteed to get laughed at. She stuffed her gym clothes in her backpack; and cautiously peeked out from behind the door from the bathroom. Lucky for her, the hallways were empty. Sophie just wanted to go home, it was almost impossible for her to think straight, her legs were shaky, and her voice was dry. *What a fucking bastard.* Sophie wiped her face with her sweater sleeve.

The next day, Sophie was sitting in class; her mind was still stuck on yesterday. No matter what she did to keep her mind occupied, her mind still wandered back in the arms of the past.

"Has anyone seen Chris?" The teacher asked, with a clipboard in her hand. The room fell quiet and people exchanged stares. The classroom door opened, in walked Chris with a white slip in his hand, his left arm was in an arm cast. Chris walked to his seat, people stared at him giggling. Sophie looked up at him, and his lip looked swollen, and his right eye was black. On his left cheek was a red mark of a Chinese symbol.

I guess that's why they say Karma's a bitch. Sophie turned back around satisfied.

"Hey man…what happened to you?" A guy sitting a few seats away from Sophie asked.

"I saved some kittens." Chris mumbled.

"What?"

"I saved some kittens." He mumbled again

"Dude I can't hear a word you're saying speak up." His friend tapped him on the arm lightly.

"I got hit by a train! Ok?! That's what happened!" Chris bellowed. His friend put both his hands up. "Alright man chill."

After class was over Chris approached Sophie blocking her path.

"Hey um...I'm sorry about yesterday..." Chris looked down at the ground avoiding eye contact with her.

"Oh...it's ok..." Sophie said softly. Chris hurriedly left the room. She began to wonder if Chris just fell or something, but then there was that weird mark on his cheek. But what surprised her even more, is that she actually felt sorry for him. Sophie knew she shouldn't have and what goes around comes around, but the look on Chris's face was just blank to her. It looked like he just went through a life changing experience, literally, and at any moment he would just fall to his knees and cry. But her sympathy was overtaken by the sequence of events from yesterday and all the feelings of pain, embarrassment, and sadness came rushing back to her. Sophie closed her eyes hearing all of the laughing, seeing all of the stares, and seeing no one in site to defend her. Those words Chris had said, ringing in her ear like a snake of the devil. Sophie opened her eyes. She was thinking what was done was done, and what was yesterday, is certainly not today. Sophie went home that day feeling content.

Blah, Blah, Blah, is all Sophie could hear Marribell saying during lunch. Sophie kept rolling her orange around on the table finding that more fascinating than listening to Marribell's nonsense. She missed Vermyear in a way; she missed having butlers at lunch and the nice calming classical music that played over the intercom during passing period. Sophie closed her eyes reminiscing about symphony number 5 in her head. A loud bell, for the gym class, cut her fantasy short making her remember where she was. The bell dragged on and on until it died down into quietness.

Oh great, even the bell died, how am I suppose to survive?

"And he like tried to kiss me, isn't that stupid? I mean my gravy, we've been broken off for a while and then he's gonna try to kiss me? Isn't that stupid?" Marribell finished.

"Yup, sure is." Sophie stated plainly.

"I know he had the nerve to try with me."

Sophie took a sigh and looked the other way wishing she could shoot herself. Marribell nudged Sophie.

"Hey did you wanna hang out later on this week?"

"No." *No way am I gonna hang out with her after what happened last time, that was just a bunch of crap right there.*

Marribell looked confused. "Why not jelly bean?"

What is wrong with this girl? Sophie had to think quick for a good enough excuse.

Think, think, think, umm…I could say I have a funeral to go to. No I can't say that because then she'd probably ask who died. I know! Maybe I can tell her I have a lot of homework. No, because then she'd wanna come over and study and bother me at my house. Hmm… or I could just say I already have plans. Yeah that's good enough.

"I have plans with someone already so…"

"Oh, you do? Who is it?" Maybe we all can hang out."

"Are you stupid?

"Huh?" Marribell titled her head confused.

"No we're not all hanging out, this is mine and the other person's plans, and you are nowhere involved.

"Well excuuuuse me, I was just offering."

"Well I don't want your offer."

Marribell turned the other way and began another conversation with someone else. Sophie glanced around the room still wishing she could go back to some place familiar. She just wanted to get up and out of this school.

'Truth'

Alexander

Sophie didn't know what he wanted. He was everywhere. His essence, his mystery, and his name in her ear giving her a kiss every night she laid her head down. Marribell was right; there was something strange about Entino Auwz. But everyone has a shadow including Sophie that she never rattled. She would spend endless hours staring off into space thinking about him, and how lustful Entino made her feel no matter where she was. But how could he have this much effect on her, and he didn't even know her, at least she thought. Whenever Sophie would run into him standing in the hallway, one foot up against the lockers smoking; she never felt so dangerously desired and liked it this much. Whatever he wanted from her, she didn't care just as long as he wanted her. But Sophie knew soon enough these lustful thoughts, or feelings she had towards him would eventually subside; she would want something tangible. At first, Sophie found it impossible for any other guy to replace Slyder's presence, until now.

Sophie opened her locker when she suddenly was startled by Marribell annoyingly smacking on a piece of gum.

"Hey Gribso, whatcha doin?"

I swear if this girl says one more thing to me I think I will make that shot of bleach with a side of anti freeze. And if that doesn't work, I'll throw myself off a cliff.

"Um...I'm putting my books away."

Marribell kept smacking on her gum and placed her hand on her hip nodding her head.

"Are you lost? Do you need something?" Sophie asked her closing her locker.

Marribell stopped smacking for a moment and thought about it.

"Hmm...no I don't think so." Marribell gave a smile.

Sophie rolled her eyes.

"Hey did you wanna hang out at my place after school with my friend?" Marribell asked following Sophie.

Sophie's eyes became slanted.

"Um...no."

"Why don't you ever wanna hang out with me?"

"Because you're embarrassing."

"How? We're not goin anywhere public. We're gonna be at my house silly goose." Marribell stopped walking and Sophie did the same.

"I promise I won't do anything embarrassing. I'll text you later alligator!" Marribell then skipped off in the opposite direction after having bellowed her embarrassing statement in front of a hallway full of students. Sophie quickly walked away to avoid any awkward stares.

"Ok here's the deal artichoke, we're gonna go to my friend's house and hang out. Because no one's home at my house. Is that a deal?" Marribell said over the phone driving on her way to Sophie's house.

"Yeah sure whatever."

"Okie doke, see ya when I get there."

Sophie just hung up the phone without saying anything waiting to be embarrassed once again. Marribell rang the door bell once they arrived to their destination. Sophie noticed on the door knob was the same Chinese symbol that was imbedded on Chris's cheek.

Wait...but how did...what was Chris even doing here anyway?

"Hold on a second." A faint voice said from behind the door.

While Sophie and Marribell were waiting, Sophie looked some more at her surroundings. Everything looked normal except she's never seen a house painted as light blue as this one. But she liked the fact it was the only house that stood out aside from all the others on the block. Sophie suddenly heard all this clanking and chains behind the door and it quickly opened.

"Hey Marribell, come in come in."

Great another weird girl to worry about.

"Hey Charlie, this is my cousin Sophia, but everyone calls her Sophie."

Charlie ran her fingers through her short brown hair.

"Hey Sophie."

"Hey."

Charlie gave a smile.

"So, where's that game you said you wanted to play?"

"Oh yeah…I was looking for it all day but I couldn't find it. I think it's somewhere upstairs."

"Ok we'll help you come look, come on Soph." Marribell hurried up the stairs.

Sophie took her time.

"But what game did you want me to look for?" She asked.

"Um…I think it's the new edition of Monopoly." Marribell said looking in some cabinets.

"Hey Sophie, why don't you look in my brothers' room, maybe it's in there somewhere." Charlie said brushing past her to go into another room to look.

"Where's his room?"

"It's right here babe." Charlie said opening a bedroom door for her.

Sophie gave an awkward smile.

"Thanks." Was all Sophie could think of to say.

"No problem Soph." Charlie smiled and went back down the hallway.

Why did she call me that?

Sophie left the door a jar behind her. The room was lit up from the sun shining through the blinds. But for some reason there was a candle lit. Sophie looked to her right and saw what looked like voodoo dolls with their mouths stitched up lining the back wall. Not far from them was a ballerina statue curtsying with her head missing.

Damn, her brother must be a freak and pretty messed up. I'm kinda scared to even look around for that dumb Monopoly game. As far as I'm concerned that game was probably sacrificed.

Sophie turned the other way and let out a gasp. There were pictures of corpses and deformed children lining the walls of his room. Sophie covered her mouth in shock.

Yeah…it looks like I got a real freak on my hands.

In the midst of all this freakiness, what was the most puzzling was a red rose lying on a night stand with a white table cloth. Lying next to the rose was the book, *The Virgin Blue by Tracy Chevalier.* Sophie picked the book up to get a closer look. She studied it for a moment flipping through the pages one by one.

"Hey Entino! Did you see that Monopoly game anywhere?!" Sophie heard Charlie cry out.

Shit shit shit. Sophie frantically put the book down hurrying over to the closet on the far side of the room and hid. Through the wooden slits, she saw Entino walk in. He took one last drag of his cigarette and put it out. Sophie observed Entino slipping his shirt off, to Sophie's surprise, he had more muscle than she thought, but not as much as Slyder.

Entino pulled out a white paper bag sitting on his bed getting out what looked like tobacco.

She saw him rolling up something and Entino placed what he rolled up in his mouth lighting it.

Typical, I knew he was on drugs.

Sophie backed away from the door further into the closet. She felt like she was trying to go into Narnia. The presence of the smoke came rushing past her once she had seen Entino walk over to the closet.

Oh crap crap.

Sophie felt like she was in one of those horror films like the Nightmare on Elm Street. The closet was almost always the place where people usually hide from a predator. She felt stupid because she always used to make fun of the people who hid in closets in scary movies, and now she was one of them. But this wasn't a scary movie, it was reality.

Why am I even in here? I'm a guest.

With each step came a creak of the floor, and along with more smoke. Sophie was breathing heavily trying not to make too much noise hoping that Entino wouldn't open the closet. But Sophie knew the odds of that happening were against her. Entino opened his closet door. He saw Sophie hugging her knees against bunches of clothes and garbage bags. And shockingly enough, Entino didn't really seem he cared she was there. It almost seemed like he was expecting her to be there. He held out his hand and helped her get to her feet. His eyes roamed her body from head to toe. Sophie's eyes remained still as a statue. She felt like she couldn't move no matter how much she wanted to or tried to. She bit her lip as Entino's arm brushed past her silky hair reaching for a light blue over shirt.

He took a drag of his cigarette.

"What do you want?" The smoke followed his words.

Sophie's body was given the ability to move again.

"Uh…I was in here because um…" Her palms were sweaty rubbing them together. "Because I was looking for something…"

Entino's eyes narrowed like he was trying to read her mind and figure her out the cigarette hanging out of his mouth like buckwheat. His eyes darted to her hands grinding together. Then he looked her in the eye.

"What were you looking for?"

"Well…actually Charlie sent me in here to look for a game. She said it might be…" Her voice trailed off.

Entino's finger tips were surfing through her long auburn hair, but his eyes were occupied with hers. Sophie broke eye contact looking down at the floor.

Oh, my gosh…he's gonna make a doll out of me.

"She said it might be in here." She finished.

His fingertips left her hair stranded on her shoulders taking a drag of his cigarette again.

"You won't find it in here."

Sophie met his eyes.

"Oh…ok…well I'll just te-.

"Hey artichoke! How's it goin?" Marribell cut Sophie off strolling into the room.

"Uh…fine…what are you doing here?" Sophie said strongly through her teeth.

Marribell laughed.

"Oh, you silly girl I came in here to check on you. Hey Entino. Di-di-di- did you find the game?" Marribell finished with a stutter.

Sophie closed her eyes shut for a moment trying her best to pretend that Marribell wasn't really here. She was like a roach that you could never just get rid of, or an obnoxious child making a scene in public at the wrong place at the wrong time.

Entino moved away from Sophie giving Marribell a nod. Sophie felt like she was drowning in a sea of embarrassment.

Marribell moved closer to Sophie.

"As you probably have heard, Sophie and I are cousins. Isn't that right Soph?" Marribell put one arm around Sophie's shoulders like they were best buds.

"Yup...so I've heard."

Entino sounded even more annoyed than Sophie was.

"Com'on Soph, Charlie's downstairs she found something else we could do."

"Ok...just...go ill meet you down there." Sophie said her face still covered under her hand.

"Okie dokie artichokie!" Marribell skipped out of the room leaving the awkward moment hanging over Sophie's head like a chandelier and surrounding Entino like a cocoon.

Right after Marribell was out of sight Sophie blurted,

"Sorry...she's... a little weird..."

Entino nodded in agreement folding his arms.

Sophie put her hands in her pockets and left the room, the awkward moment tailgating her.

The next day, Ginger had made plans with Sophie and told her to meet her at the corner 7-11.

Comeon, where is she? I've been waiting out here for half an hour.

Sophie kept looking at the time on her phone more cars passing by increasingly.

Whatever, screw this, I'm gonna go get me a drink.

Sophie walked over to the slushy machine and made herself a beverage. She saw a teenage couple goofing off and laughing in the aisle next to her. The girl was recognizable; the only name Sophie knew her by was Trish. She had dropped out of Vermyear Academy and moved in with her boyfriend Rob. He was moving his big bear hands across the lining of her black mini skirt and tugging at her black leggings. Trish had a whole line of hickeys across her neck and Sophie gave a dirty looking drinking her slush.

"Hey what the fuck are you lookin at?" Rob said to Sophie.

Trish peered from behind her dark purple furred hoodie coat straight in Sophie's direction.

"Huh? What are you lookin at?" Rob said once more, this time slowly making his way over to Sophie.

Trish laid her bony fragile hand on Rob's chest stopping him.

"Comeon Rob, don't let's just go come on. We can just steal some from somewhere else."

Rob had stopped walking, but still had his eye on Sophie.

"Rob!...lets...go..." Trish demanded, this time, pulling Rob along down the aisle.

Something had fallen out of Rob's back pocket. Sophie looked to see what is was and saw it was a Trojan Condom pack.

At least they're not procreating. .

Sophie stepped her shoe right on it walking up to the front counter and paid for her drink. While the cashier was getting her change, Sophie came across a poster on the wall with a picture of a girl smiling and playing with a dog that read MISSING.

"Yup...she's been missing for a little while now." The man's scratchy voice added.

Sophie saw that someone had scratched off her name in pen.

"What was her name?" Sophie asked taking her change placing it in her pocket.

"Her name was Morgan Stasney."

Sophie looked at the picture once more; she'd never seen or heard of Morgan before. But from the looks of it, she could tell Morgan was as innocent as any other missing person. She wondered what her life would be like if Morgan and she ever became best friends. Sophie knew she'd be a better friend than Ginger ever could be.

"It's sad isn't it?" The man behind the counter interrupted Sophie's train of thought.

"Yeah..." Sophie agreed taking her slushy and thanking him. She thought that Ginger would be there by now, but of course she was a no show.

Sophie was walking back towards the parking lot, when she bumped into Slyder.

Her heart restarted itself.

"I'll call you back, bye." He hung up the phone.

Sophie gave a smile placing her hair back behind her ear.

"Hey Sophie, I haven't seen you in a while." Slyder pulled her in for a warm embrace.

"I know." Sophie wrapped her arms tightly around his neck, his muscular upper body gently touching her.

"How've you been, I missed you." Slyder asked walking down the street with her.

"I've...been alright I guess. How bout you?"

Slyder shrugged.

"Well...I guess I've been alright as well."

They both stopped walking. Sophie just gave a pleasant smirk.

"Where've you been?"

Sophie looked up at him.

"What do you mean?"

"I mean just what I said, where've you been? You just vanished."

"Oh, well I transferred so..." Sophie's voice became quiet.

"Where to?"

"Cornegy." Sophie said, not looking him in the eye. She felt ashamed and embarrassed to admit it.

"Ah...I see." Slyder took her hand and caressed it.

"So...has Vermyear Academy changed at all?" They continued to walk down the street together hand in hand.

"No, not really, it's just lonely there. You know I didn't even know you left. I thought you were sick or something or maybe went on vacation somewhere and you were coming back."

Sophie let out a laugh.

"I wish that were the case."

She felt important and needed. She had no idea that Slyder had missed her this much, or had even thought about her since she left. Sophie held on to his hand tight not wanting to let go.

"We really need to keep in contact and see each other more often because I can't have you vanish from me again." He gave a warm smile and pulled her close once more and stroked her soft auburn hair. This is where Sophie wanted to be, right in Slyder's arms where she belonged. She nestled him under his neck, and he stroked her back.

"I'll text you, and maybe we can hang out this weekend, or next weekend or something? How's that sound?" Slyder whispered in her ear holding her close.

Sophie smiled her heart racing fast like a cheetah.

"Yeah…I'd like that." Sophie finally got her wish and felt like one of those Disney princesses in movies.

And before Sophie knew it, the weekend had begun, and Slyder had told Sophie to meet him in front of the main entrance of the mall.

She texted him back with a smiley face.

"Boo." Slyder whispered into her ear from behind.

Sophie turned around and smiled getting pulled in close to him with a hug.

He took her hand leading her into the mall. In a way, Sophie felt lucky to be hand in hand with Slyder at the mall on a Friday night where most people from their schools hung out and they would be seen together. She remembered always coming to the mall seeing young teen couples coming to the mall together laughing and enjoying each other's company. She wondered if she'd ever get to experience something like that one day, but tonight her wait was over.

'Roy'

Lights out Asia

"Alright so how much do we know about the case?" Detective Roy's boss asked standing in the door way of her office.

"Well...we know that this girl named Morgan Stasney has been missing for two days. But right now, we don't have any leads." Detective Roy crossed her arms leaning back in her chair.

Her boss pinched the bridge of her nose letting out a frustrated sigh.

"But...I'm gathering a search team together to go and search for some more clues." Roy added, trying to reassure her.

"Alright, just do what you have to do"

Her boss walked out of the office.

Roy was becoming anxious. She had no leads, and from the looks of it wasn't going to get any any time soon. She opened her drawer and pulled out the picture of Morgan that was on almost every MISSING poster in town. Roy would often look at her picture from time to time as if that would some how lead her to where Morgan was. Roy just didn't understand, Morgan looked so happy and content with her life with a smile so pretty and bright why would she ever want to vanish?

"Where are you?" Roy whispered to herself running her thumb across Morgan's face and her dog.

A sudden knock at the door made her jump.

"Bad time?" Her partner, Jack Stewart, asked with a cup of coffee in his hand.

Roy quickly placed the photo back in the drawer slamming it shut giving a smile.

"No I was just looking over some things. That's all." She folded her hands together on her desk with a clutter of papers.

"Well I was just gonna go to the café to get something to snack on, wanna join?"

Roy tapped her fingers on her desk for a second thinking.

"Uh sure why not?"

They walked out of the office together side by side.

"So, anything new with the case yet?" Jack asked taking a sip of his coffee.

Roy shook her head.

"No, but I was gonna head out and do some more questioning. I mean there has to be something we're missing, because otherwise it just doesn't make sense."

After purchasing their snacks, they both sat at a table together.

"I mean...I don't know Jack, there's just something that doesn't seem right. I mean how could a girl who had everything going for her, everything in her life perfect just disappear like this?"

Jack raised his eyebrows while drinking some more of his coffee.

"I don't know Roy I mean everyone is just as confused as you are. You see with cases like this, nothing really makes sense. No one is gonna make sense of this, no one but us."

Roy looked down at her sandwich but didn't say anything. Jack was right, it was their job to make sense of other people's mess in their lives no matter how pointless or hopeless the right answer seemed. She wanted to help Morgan, her family, and her friends all find out what really happened. All of them were depending on her to give them closure. But how could someone who was as clueless as you are, possibly provide that?

Roy and her partner arrived at Morgan's parents' house. The house looked quiet and still from the last time they were here. The whole block was for that matter. No kids playing in the yard, no dogs barking, no people walking. It was like the ghost town in all of Connecticut. Roy knocked on the door. She could hear a dog begin to bark faintly in the background and footsteps hurrying to the door. A woman with brown hair pinned back peered from behind the door.

"Yes?" She said quietly.

"Mrs. Stasney, detective Roy and my partner Jack." They both held up their badges against the screen door.

"We're here to ask you a few questions you mind if we could come in for a minute?"

Mrs. Stasney remained quiet and nodded allowing them to step into the threshold. The Golden Retriever that had been barking ran up to them wagging its tail its tongue sticking out. Roy immediately recognized the dog from the pictures posted of Morgan on almost every corner.

"Sorry I was just…um…packing up some of Morgan's things…" Her voice grew quiet again, tears rolling down her bony face.

Roy cleared her throat piercing her lips together while she and Jack sat on the two chairs across from the sofa a glass table separating them from Mrs. Stasney. She wiped her tears away from her blood shot eyes. She looked pale, empty, and washed out.

"So, um what did you come here to ask me?"

Roy placed her hair behind her ear.

"Well, um we came here to ask you some more about the day or the day before Morgan went missing. Do you mind telling us from start to finish of how the morning or the morning before had gone one more time just to make sure we didn't miss anything?" Roy took out a pad a paper and a pen preparing to take some notes.

Mrs. Stasney eyes became a fountain, overflowed with tears and she looked up at the ceiling trying her best to keep them from falling away from her blank eyes.

"Well…um…the morning before she went missing, we uh… well…the whole family my husband Morgan and I had gone out for dinner. And…I don't think…anything out of the ordinary happened. We came home, she said she was tired and went up stairs to go to sleep. And that's all I remember happening that day." She wiped her face some more sniffling.

"Well how bout the day of?" Jack asked leaning on the edge of his seat.

"Well I remember I got up that morning pretty early because

I had to take Morgan to cheerleading practice. And then she told me that…after practice she was gonna go to her friend's house." Mrs. Stasney began to sob bearing her face in a pillow. "And then…I never saw her again after that. That was the last time I ever saw her." She continued to sob.

Roy looked over at Jack who was looking back at her.

"Mrs. Stasney, um…do you remember what time you dropped her off at cheerleading practice and when it ended?" Roy asked leaning more on the edge of her seat taking some notes.

Mrs. Stasney shook her head.

"But…" She mumbled under her trembling hands.

"But what?" Roy eagerly asked.

"I still have the schedule hanging up on the refrigerator in the kitchen." Mrs. Stasney pointed and Roy was already headed in that direction. She looked at the refrigerator that had the schedule stuck to it.

"What day was it Mrs. Stasney do you remember?" Roy yelled from the kitchen.

"It was a Tuesday. The last day of the month."

Roy looked at the time; practice was from 8 o'clock in the morning to 2 o'clock in the afternoon. She instantly took some more notes rushing back into the living room.

"Mrs. Stasney, I remember you mentioned she was going over to a friend's house, who are they? What is their name?"

Mrs. Stasney continued to sob in her pillow for a moment, but Roy waited patiently for an answer. Suddenly the door opened and the dog began to bark again.

"Shut up fee fee!" A tall man well built entered and closed the creaking door behind him. He stopped dead in his tracks once he saw Roy and Jack sitting in the living room.

"What the hell is this?"

"Mr. Stasney I'm sorry to bother you but we're just here to-"

"I know why you're here; you won't leave us the hell alone. I told you Barbra not to bring these fucking cops back into our house. I told you! Why don't you ever listen to me?" He pointed at his wife yelling over Roy's head.

Mrs. Stasney's head shot up from the soaking wet pillow, her eyes baggy and pink.

"What the hell else was I suppose to do Rick?! No one else is gonna help us find out what happened! Are you gonna go out there and find out what happened to her Rick?! Huh? Are you?!" She wailed her arms around in anger.

"Hey, you shut the hell up Barbra. We all know damn well you ain't gonna go out there and look for her either." He pointed at her once more and then looked down at Roy.

"And you can get the hell out of my way." Rick shoved Roy to the side. Jack stood up edging over to the both of them.

"Hey! Don't you ever put your hands on me like that again do you understand?"

Rick's construction boots stopped scrubbing against the peeling wood floor. He turned to face her, his peppered black hair twinkling in the sun light beaming through the thin white curtains.

"You just get the hell out of my house. If you come back here again, then you might as well just consider yourself missing too."

Roy sarcastically nodded her head and smiled.

"Is that uh, a threat Mr. Stasney?" Roy questioned him pulling back her light navy blue over coat revealing her gun tucked into a holster.

Mr. Stasney glanced down at it and smiled. His dark eyes darted back up at her.

"As a matter of fact, yes it was. Now get…the…hell…out…of… my…house." He disappeared into the hallway throwing his red plaid over shirt down as he went. Roy looked back at Barbra who was still sitting there wiping her face. Jack rushed over to her and kneeled beside her.

"Mrs. Stasney," He began laying a hand on her shoulder. "We really need you to tell us the name of Morgan's friend she was gonna go see. And the address if possible." He spoke softly.

Mrs. Stasney shook her head and buried it in her hands.

"I… I…can't remember…" She mumbled.

Roy rushed over there to them both.

"Mrs. Stasney please try to remember, for your daughter's sake."

Roy begged softly.

Mrs. Stasney's eyes were still for a minute, and then suddenly she inhaled deeply her pale green eyes seemed to look alive again.

"It was her friend Tracey I think it was. Yeah…that was what she told me."

Roy frantically handed Mrs. Stasney the pad of paper and pen.

"Write it down, the address. Please. Quickly." Roy said to her.

Mrs. Stasney began to fumble around with the pen trying to get a good grip. It was difficult for her because her hands were all shaky and sweaty.

"Barbra! If those cops are still here…" Mr. Stasney's voice trailed off, but Roy could hear him thumping down the stairs into the gloomy dark hallway.

"Please quickly!" Roy said her heart beating fast.

Mrs. Stasney's handwriting was a little bit like chicken scratch could you blame her? But even so, it was still easy to read.

"Barbra!" Mr. Stasney yelled once more, the footsteps becoming louder. Roy could feel his dark shadow hurryingly nearing them.

She kept looking behind her shoulder, Jack was biting his lip and even he began to sweat.

Just as Mrs. Stasney finished scribbling it down, she immediately handed it back to Roy and in walked Mr. Stasney.

"I thought I told you to get the hell out of here!" Mr. Stasney pointed towards the door. Roy quickly and discreetly slipped Mrs. Stasney her business card.

"Oh, don't worry Mr. Stasney we are." Roy said with Jack following her out of the house the screen door slamming behind them.

'Knocked up'

Kings of Leon & Lykke Li

"How are you doing honey?" Ginger's mother came and sat down beside Ginger on her bed. Ginger's eyes slowly opened.

"I still feel sick." Ginger wiped the sleep away from her eyes.

Her mother smoothed Ginger's hair back from out of her face and gave a smile.

"Are you still vomiting?"

Ginger laid her hand on her forehead letting out a sigh.

"Yeah I'm vomiting here and there."

"Maybe its just food poisoning, you think?" Her mother continued to stroke her hair back. "After all, you did eat a lot of food at your Aunt's get together last night."

Ginger shrugged.

"I don't know mom, I just want it to stop. I was supposed to meet Drew today to hang out." Ginger sounded disappointed.

Her mother shook her head.

"I'm sorry sweetie, but it looks like you're gonna have to hang out with him a different day." Her mother stood up walking over to Ginger's dresser getting the thermometer and walking back over to Ginger.

"Here. Let's take your temperature." Her mother held it up to her mouth, but Ginger shook her head fanning it away.

"Come on honey please?" Her mother begged.

Ginger sighed taking the thermometer popping it in her mouth. Seconds later it began to beep.

"Hm…that's strange…your temperature is normal." Her mother said her eyebrows making a confused expression.

"See?" Ginger suddenly boasted. "I'm fine; if I feel sick or I'm gonna throw up trust me Drew and I will take care of it."

Her mother laughed a little setting the thermometer down on the dresser.

"Please mom, can I go? Please? I'd hate to stand him up." Ginger pleaded, already slipping out of her cozy bed. Her mother folded her arms pondering weather or not to let her daughter go tapping her foot on the white shag carpet.

"Alright…fine, you can go. BUT…you have to promise me if you ever at any point feel nauseous or faint, I want you to tell Drew to take you straight home got it?"

Ginger nodded her head in agreement quickly getting dressed.

A few minutes later Drew was outside waiting for her in his pick up truck.

Ginger hurriedly got in the car and gave him a kiss on the lips.

"Hey." He smiled at her backing out of the driveway.

"Hi." She blushed and smiled at him.

"How are you feeling?" He asked one hand on the steering wheel and the other rubbing her thigh up to the cut of her blue jean shorts.

Ginger smiled again.

"I'm…ok I still felt a little faint and nauseous earlier though but I'm alright."

Drew smiled at her, "That's good, you mind if I make a quick stop over to the convenient store real quick? I wanna to get a bag of sun flower seeds."

"Oh go right ahead."

Drew parked his truck in front of the double glass doors.

"Be right back babe won't take long." He quickly got out of the car, his messy short brown hair blowing in the wind. Ginger sat in the car looking out the window waiting. She was hoping that she didn't get sick any time soon because she wanted to enjoy the time spent with Drew. He came out a few minutes later jogging back to the truck.

And suddenly, Ginger began to feel nauseated again. She covered her mouth up opening the door.

"Where you goin'?" Drew asked opening his bag of seeds.

"I'll be back." Ginger answered quickly.

Drew put his bag down.

"Let me come with you." Drew offered about to open the door as well when Ginger stopped him.

"No no no, I'm fine, just stay here." She closed the door running into the store heading straight for the bathroom. She busted through the heavy metal door and didn't even bother to lock it, falling to her knees slightly skidding across the hard floor her head over the toilet bowl. She brushed her loose curly hair out from her face panting and breathing heavily but nothing happened. Ginger felt better and she was glad. She took a deep breath and got to her feet dusting herself off gathering her composure. She saw herself in the mirror taking a step back to look at her body shape and curves. Ginger patted her hair down fixing it back up and walked out of the bathroom. She passed through the aisle that had Trojan's and pregnancy tests. Ginger stopped walking taking a few steps back looking at the shelf again. She was thinking about buying a pregnancy test. But she wasn't pregnant; but she knew she was trying to convince herself that was true. Ginger never thought she'd ever have to question that. But here she was, doing the one thing she never thought possible. She bit her lip and quickly glanced around the bright sun lit store.

She snatched the pink rectangular box from the shelf. How was she going to have the guts to pay for this? Surely it was affordable for her, but if she went up there to the counter paying for it she'd feel dirty. She remembered watching a commercial on television about teen pregnancy. The speaker was of a girl in a black and white tint with long wavy hair that looked younger than Ginger that said: *It could happen to anyone. Don't think 'it can't happen to me.' I said the same thing once and now look at me. Don't assume you're immune.* Throughout the whole commercial the young girl didn't smile once. But then again, what was there to smile about? Ginger imaged in her mind the young girl, with her protruding belly standing over her like a mountain saying the very words she had said on the commercial. Ginger placed the box on her chest taking a long sigh making her way up to the small cluttered counter.

There was a girl with long black hair that looked close to Ginger's age smacking obnoxiously on a piece of bubble gum. Ginger slowly placed the box face down on the counter. The girl smiled through her smacks ringing her up and giving her her change. Ginger placed her change in her back pocket taking the box heading back towards the bathroom when she heard the girl behind the counter say:

"I hope you have a nice day."

Ginger ignored her comment walking into the bathroom this time locking the door behind her. She sat on the toilet opening the box up, looking at the object that would soon tell her her fate. Ginger took a sigh and began to take the test hoping that the answer wouldn't come out positive. If it did, how would she tell Drew? What would he say? How would he feel? All of those thoughts came rushing into Ginger's head all at once as she flushed the toilet holding on tightly to the test. Ginger waited there after washing her hands for the white little slot to give her a sign that could make or break her whole day, and even her whole relationship with Drew.

Seconds later, she began to see a sign appearing in the slot. Ginger held it up so that it was eye level with her, her whole body was shaking and her face became red. And that's when she saw it, the sign she'd hope not to. The pink plus sign was like an avalanche burying her all over, with no where to go swallowing her whole. Ginger swallowed hard quickly tossing it in the trash walking out of the bathroom. She passed by the girl at the counter who was still smacking obnoxiously on her gum and twirling a long black strand of her hair around her index finger. The girl gave a fake smile.

"Bye have a nice day."

Ginger walked out and saw Drew sitting in the car chewing on his seeds.

"Hey, you ok?" He asked her as she was closing the car door.

Ginger sat there in silence staring out through the windshield wishing someone else was in her spot looking from the outside in.

The words from the commercial she used to think were stupid were defining her life. Every single word was like a slap in the face saying 'wake up you're one of them now.' Ginger pinched her eyes shut not wanting to think that but she knew it was true. She was just another teenager adding to the statistic no parent wants their child to be part of and certainly not hers. Ginger felt numb stinging through her seven layers of skin all the way down to her core just eating away all of her feeling.

"Babe?" Drew said laying a hand on her shoulder.

Ginger's body twitched.

"Yeah…sorry I…was just thinking." She tried her best to smile.

"Well put your seat belt on babe, you're not immune."

Ginger quickly looked over at him slowly placing the seat belt around her. Her eyes became like a squirrels. Her body was tense, and she began to sweat feeling her heart drum out an echo through her ears, her white tank top absorbing her sticky skin.

"Can we just…get out of here? I just wanna relax and clear my mind."

Drew smiled.

"Alright." He said starting up the car backing out heading further down the black top road.

Drew stopped near a creek underneath a shade of an oak tree. He rolled down the windows allowing the sounds of birds and leaves bristling in the wind to surround them. She laid there with her eyes closed thinking about what the test had read. Ginger began to doubt it and think maybe she read it wrong, or maybe it was broken. But none of that really made any sense. She laid her hand on her flat stomach that would soon turn into a huge hill that would take nine months of her life to get rid of, and the rest of her life to raise. She opened her eyes when she felt Drew begin to kiss her neck moving over on the passenger side of the truck. She lifted his head wrapping her legs around him kissing his lips his breath smelled like sunflower seeds. Drew's hands started to roam her body like a map and he began to unzip her shorts when Ginger laid her hand on his to stop him.

"No Drew…not today." Ginger looked away from him.

"Why, are you on your monthly again?" Drew asked leaning some of his weight off of her. Was this her time to tell him? Or should she keep it to herself until she began to show. But Ginger knew that wouldn't be fair to him because he had a right to know just as much as she did. But she was scared, how was she going to tell him. She just couldn't think of the right words to say. She looked over at him and caressed his smooth face and smiled.

"No." Her voice quiet shaking her head.

Drew pulled her in tight and kissed her on the forehead. Ginger rested in his arms locked around her waist knowing soon she'd be a mother, and Drew as of right now didn't know he'd be a father. But she didn't care what anyone said, she was going to have his baby.

'Will you find me'

Mai

Morgan Stasney was out there somewhere. But the obvious question is where? The missing posters plastered on every wall, dancing pointlessly on every street, and stapled on every phone wire pole was just another posing question at hand: If Morgan Stasney is still alive, would you find her? Roy didn't believe so. With most MISSING person cases, if you are unable to find them in the next 48 hours, the likelihood of them still breathing are very slim. Roy felt like she was looking for a ghost. She didn't have faith that Morgan was still alive at all she's been missing for over a week. But when she saw Mrs. Stasney and how desperate she was, and how Mr. Stasney was beginning to give up on his only daughter that was enough motivation to keep a little bit of faith inside of her.

"Well it's a good thing we have the keys to Morgan's car." Roy stated opening the passenger side door. She slipped on some latex gloves and started rummaging around sifting through receipts, makeup, and chips.

"She sure wasn't neat." Jack observed searching the back seats and Roy snickered.

"That's an understatement." She quickly glanced at everything she picked up seeing if it would have any connection to Morgan's disappearance.

"It all just looks like trash and junk." Jack stated still searching.

"Well there has to be something." Roy picked up what looked

like a regular book from the library but she turned it over and saw the words, 'Diary'. "Well this might come in handy." She showed it to Jack who looked relieved.

"Well that's great we found something."

"But let's keep looking." She said and she picked up a silver necklace with a heart and key dangling. "Hmm, well it appears she may have had a boyfriend or a love interest." The heart swung slowly turning and Roy saw two letters engraved on it, S&M "Well it's obvious the M was her name, but who's the S for?"

"Who knows…Sam, Shawn maybe?" Jack exclaimed.

"Could be…well…I checked everything up here. What about you?" Roy questioned gathering her discovered potential evidence.

"Yes, I looked at everything back here. We could have the forensic analysts dust for any finger prints. See if we can lift anything."

Roy started flipping through the diary looking for anything that stood out. But nothing caught her eye, it was just the typical teenage girl things, crushes, teachers she didn't like, friends she didn't like, and what she wished her life was like. She put it away so she could examine it later.

"Let's follow this lead Ms. Stasney gave us for now." Roy suggested. They drove around neighborhoods looking for the address Mrs. Stasney had scribbled down.

"I hope she's home I'd hate to go through all of this trouble and she's not there." Roy said looking down at the yellow lined paper.

Jack smiled and shook his head turning down another street.

"Don't worry Roy, she'll be there, and if she's not well then I'm sure we can just come back another time." Jack reassured her.

Roy shrugged, still anxious for answers.

"Yeah I guess you're right." Jack drove past several houses when Roy startled him.

"Hold on stop! This is it…this is the address she wrote." Roy placed her hand tightly on Jack's sleeve of his suit. He pulled the car over onto the side of the road next to the curb. He turned to look out the back window.

"Are you sure that's the house back there?" Jack gestured to where he was looking.

"Yes, I'm positive come on let's go." Roy got out of the car with Jack closely following behind. This block looked empty and still like the Stasney's residence. But Roy knew soon enough that the stillness in the air would be familiar and normal to everyone who lived here until justice for Morgan eliminated it. Jack rang the doorbell. They didn't hear anyone inside moving. Jack rang the door bell once more and the door opened and appeared a slim teenage girl with brown pig tails.

"Hi Tracey?" Jack asked.

The girl nodded her head.

"Hi, I'm detective Stewart and this is my partner Roy, we're just here to ask you a few questions you mind if we come in for a minute?" Jack and Roy put their badges away.

Tracey let them come in and they both took a seat on the couch.

"Am I in trouble?" Tracey asked sitting across from them in a love seat with one leg tucked beneath her.

Roy shook her head.

"No no, we're just gonna ask you some questions about your friend, Morgan."

"Oh…alright. So, what did you want to know?" Tracey began to pick at the skin around her nails slowly moving her hands to the tiny scab on her knobby knee.

"Alright well first of all, you were in cheer leading with her is that correct?" Roy asked her gathering out a pad of paper and a pen.

Tracey nodded.

"Alright and the day she disappeared were you there at practice?" Roy asked her.

"Yeah I never miss practice. Although…she sometimes did." Tracey looked down at the carpet, her loose strands of hair curtaining her face.

"What do you mean? Was she there most of the time though? Or…hardly ever or what?" Jack asked further.

Tracey shrugged. "She just…sometimes never showed up. But I mean she always disappears sometimes like that and when she did it wasn't like it was anything out of the ordinary because she always came back."

Roy quickly scribbled down some notes.

"Tracey, um what do you mean by disappear?"

"Like…she would just sometimes stop replying to all of her friends' messages or stop returning my calls. At first it bothered me, but then I guess I just got used to it."

Roy nodded her head writing down some more.

"And you're saying she did that often?" Roy asked trying to be certain.

"Hmmhmm." Tracey nodded.

"Ok, did you know of anyone she was dating? A boyfriend a crush anything?" Roy probed.

Tracey thought for a moment then shook her head. "No, no one comes to mind."

"Alright so what did you and Morgan do after practice was over?"

"Nothing." Tracey simply answered without hesitation in her voice this time.

"So you guys just came back to your place and did…nothing?" Jack asked confused.

Tracey shook her head. "You're confusing me."

"Didn't Morgan come over to your house after practice…?" Roy's voice became still before she could hardly get out her full sentence.

"What? No, Morgan never came to my house." Tracey answered confused lifting her head up.

Roy and Jack exchanged stares.

It didn't make sense it could either be one of three things, Tracey was lying, Morgan's mother was lying, or Morgan herself did. But if Morgan did lie, what was the reason behind it? Why didn't she just tell someone where she was really going? But then if she didn't go to Tracey's house, and she didn't go home…then where could she have gone?

"Where did she say she was going?" Jack asked as the moment of silence succumbed to his strong voice.

Tracey shrugged. "Uh…she said that she was going down to the BBQ Shack to get some dinner and then home. "And…that was the last I saw of my best friend." Tracey finished picking at her braces.

Roy gathered her belongings off the tan leather couch standing up with Jack beside her.

"Well thank you Tracey for your time, here's my business card call us if you hear or discover anything else." Jack said walking out of the house closing the door behind him.

Roy got down to the bottom of the cement steps taking a long sigh.

Jack approached behind her laying a hand on her shoulder.

"Don't worry Roy, we'll figure this out. This just needs a lot of work."

She brushed her red hair back from her face and nodded.

"So now it looks like our little victim might be a liar." Roy placed her hands on her hips walking back to the car Jack following her. He let out a laugh.

"Well what did you expect? She's a teenager, and she obviously didn't want anyone to know where she was headed."

"Well that's the next step then, the BBQ Shack, maybe someone who works there remembers her coming in."

Jack nodded in agreement and they wasted no time arriving at the eatery. Roy got out of the car observing the building and noticed that they had surveillance from a few different angles watching the parking lot and entrance. Roy glanced over at Jack and she could tell from his smirk their minds were in sync.

"Hopefully they still have the footage of that day." Roy and Jacked rushed in and saw that the restaurant wasn't that busy and Roy approached a man wiping down tables.

"Excuse me," Roy began and the man turned to face them. "I'm detective Roy and this is Jack, we were wondering if those cameras outside and I see that there are a couple in here are working?"

"Yes…why? Is there a problem officer?" The man answered.

"No it's just we need to access some footage from a particular night we're investigating a missing person." Roy pulled out the picture of Morgan showing it to the man. "Have you seen this girl here before?"

The man studied the picture holding it close to get a better look. "Hmm I'm not sure, she looks a little familiar but then again, I see a lot of people coming in and out of here." He handed the photo back.

"Well can we see if the cameras picked up anything of interest?"

Roy asked and the man gestured them to follow. He led them in the back of the restaurant unlocking a door and he presented them to the security system with two monitors that showed different angles of the outside and inside the restaurant.

"Perfect thank you, can you que up the camera from a week ago?" Roy requested as she took a seat next to the man and Jack did the same. The man did as she asked and her focus was on the cameras showing the entrance. She knew that if Tracey was telling the truth, then Morgan should show up on camera. All three of them sat in silence studying the footage.

A few minutes passed with no sign of Morgan and at first, Roy was beginning to think maybe either Morgan changed her mind and went somewhere else, or Tracey was lying. But suddenly, there she was, Morgan Stasney in living color. Finally seeing Morgan for the first time felt surreal. It wasn't often when Roy could witness what exactly happened to victims and where they were going. Her eyes were fixed on Morgan as she saw her walking towards the entrance of the restaurant. Morgan picked up her pace racing to an unknown man. They hugged and held each other having a conversation.

"Who is that?" Jack spoke softly leaning in squinting to get a better view. Roy shook her head.

"No idea. Whoever it is, they seem very comfortable with one another."

The pair strolled down the side walk out of view.

"Wait where the hell is she going?" Roy questioned baffled.

She kept watching for a few more minutes to make sure the pair weren't caught on camera one last time. But they didn't show up, at least not together. Morgan was seen again a few minutes later sprinting in the opposite direction.

"Could you rewind that a little bit?" Roy requested focusing more intensely.

The surveillance once more, displayed Morgan darting across the monitor.

"Pause it right there!" Roy ordered peering in closer. She studied the grainy still image of the frightened teenager and realized that the strap from her cheerleading uniform was snapped and torn dangling alongside her. Morgan's face was stricken with fear and seeing how terrified she was triggered an uncanny chill along Roy's spine.

"Who in the world is she running from?" Jack exclaimed. Roy could tell that he was just as anxious as she was.

"Maybe that guy she was with…but first we have to get copies of all the surveillance from every business that would be along this street and any side streets. Thank you, sir, for your time." Roy stated rushing out.

Roy stopped walking and looked up at the orange glowing sky and for the first time in all the years of her career, she was imagining herself somewhere else weightless with no problems to worry about and no crime to solve. But she knew on the teeter totter of life, reality was always more weight; restraining you back from being the one higher up.

'In Ohio on some steps'

Limbeck

Sophie was in the company of Slyder Thomas grinning up at him enjoying herself and she was glad her mother allowed her to go on a road trip with him. She had never thought in a lifetime something like this would happen. What more could a girl ask for?

"You want me to get you some more lemonade?" Slyder offered with Sophie's empty glass in his hand.

Sophie shook her head smiling. "No that's ok. But thanks anyway."

Slyder stretched out in the booth placing his hands behind his head.

"I'm sooo glad to be off, aren't you?" Slyder tried to make conversation.

"Absolutely, you don't know how tired I was."

Slyder grinned, showing his perfect white smile.

"You're funny." He told her sliding out of the booth tossing a few dollars on the table walking Sophie out of the café. The heat and wind beamed down on them both, the wind threading through Sophie's long hair. Slyder rushed up behind her like a tidal wave grabbing her waist spinning her around in his arms. Sophie shrieked, with excitement filling her voice. She slid down and Slyder nestled her neck one arm caressing her curves and the other opening the passenger side door.

Sophie giggled and smiled wanting Slyder to hold her in his arms longer. Is this what it felt like to be liked by someone? To be truly happy? To be wanted by someone? All of these questions came tumbling over Sophie's mind all at once almost making her feel light headed. But even if she did begin to stumble, Slyder was there to catch her. She slipped into the passenger seat closing the door and they continued down the lengthy road. Sophie looked out the window at all the passing cars and all the passing trees. She looked up at the beaming white clouds covered in sunlight until her eyes became watered. She turned to face Slyder seeing his golden hair mixing with the wind coming and going out of the window. She felt so content being with him in his presence. Sophie became lost in him like a maze. No matter how much she tried to figure out his true feelings for her, she'd come to a dead end. It made her angry, yet it also made her more interested in him all at the same time. She just didn't understand; he was the cause of her agony and her happiness all at once. But were they exclusive? Sophie wasn't sure.

He treated her like his girlfriend, he held her hand in public, he gave her hugs, he called her and texted her almost every morning, and he'd pay for almost every date they went on.

And all of these things left Sophie to think, 'What did he think of her?'

He turned his head slightly and smiled at her. "You ok?"

Sophie shook her head giving a smile in return.

"Yeah...I'm fine."

Slyder laid one arm around Sophie's shoulders. His touch was electrifying giving life to all of her dead ends.

'Why?' She thought to herself. Why couldn't their relationship just be like the ones Sophie read in story books? Why couldn't it be like an ordinary fairytale? The guy finds the girl, the guy falls in love with the girl they get married and have kids and that's the end of it. It was basically simple as one, two, three. So why was it so difficult for her? Surely she didn't think Slyder was playing the whole 'hard to get' thing. What was holding him back?

"We're almost there. It shouldn't be that much longer." Slyder assured her giving Sophie a smile. He glanced at her and saw a few tears trickling down Sophie's plush cheek.

"Hey, what's wrong?" Slyder pulled her in closer.

Sophie looked up at him, her eyes almost a well.

"What do you mean?"

"Well, you're crying."

Sophie immediately sat up looking in the review mirror.

"I am?" She said wiping her face with her hands.

"Yeah..." Slyder's voice trailed off. "You sure you're alright?"

Sophie just nodded her head as a response. She didn't even know she was crying. But she wasn't thinking about anything that would cause tears. Well, tears of sadness anyway. She looked in the mirror once more making sure her eye liner wasn't smeared. Leaning against the window, letting the awkwardness settle in between Slyder and her, Sophie saw a green sign that read 'Cedar Point 20 miles'.

'Searchin' For Summer'

Mike Taylor

The water washing up on the banks of shore, taking grain by grain, pebble by pebble. Laughter, and chatter fill the dense air around them fun happy chaos on every corner not a dull moment anywhere. Children eating cones of ice cream watching the entertaining parade march by while people watch in cable cars up above. The rolling thunders of the roller coasters were mixing with the screams of excitement, loop after loop. A seagull being cautious by the boardwalk, looking for scraps as the sun begins to rest, hovering over the orange horizon.

Chapter Sixteen

With her heart racing, lights flashing, and people laughing Mrs. Brenda Gribsie and the slot machine were best of friends. She never had a friend who was there for her whenever she needed them, a person to count on, or even a shoulder to lean on. Her slot machine was all that and then some. It's exactly what Brenda needed, a thing who was a good friend and also made her broke.

"Come on come on come on." Brenda pleaded fluttering her hands in excitement like a baby bird learning to fly.

Her best friend was trying to work its magic to finally put a few dollars in her wallet. Two slots were already filled with two matching cherry pairs, and all Brenda needed was a third. The slot began to slow down about to reveal the moment Brenda was hoping for. Her goggling eyes could see the cherry she needed, and her heart almost skipped a beat thinking it would stay there; but she was soon disappointed to witness the cherry go flying by and instead she got a dice. The machine let out it's whole array of happy sounds and flashing lights. Brenda banged her head against the slot machine and kicked it a few times with her black high heel. She grabbed her hand bag searching for her wallet and opening it and suddenly stopped once she saw her wallet was bone dry...once again. All she had left were coins, dimes pennies and all. Brenda slammed the clasp down on her wallet throwing it back inside her purse.

"Shit shit shit." She whispered under her breath, kicking the slot machine for a last time as a way of saying "forget you."

Brenda began to walk angrily away when she heard someone say: "You're never gonna win with that attitude."

Brenda turned to face the person. It was a tall handsome man about 6 feet with slicked back brown hair and dark blue eyes. His jaw structure was strong and firm. He took a puff of his cigar. Brenda placed her hair behind her ear.

"What...um...do you mean?"

The man smiled.

"I was watching you...from the bar and you looked like you were about to have a fit."

Brenda let out a laugh her eyes wandering up and down the man's chest.

"Well I mean, wouldn't you throw a fit if you lost to a machine?"

The man smirked once more taking another puff shaking his head.

"Nah, I play poker."

"And do you ever win?"

The man laughed.

"I'll be honest, I only lost once. That's it."

Brenda's jaw dropped.

He laughed once more.

"I'm Slate. Slate Stronghouse." He grabbed Brenda's hand and kissed it gently.

Brenda giggled and she could feel her hand turning red the minute his soft lips touched it and the redness running up her arm like an uncontrollable disease.

"I'm Brenda Gribsie."

"Well Brenda, you should come watch me play sometime."

She laughed covering her mouth while flashing her sparkling wedding ring.

"That'd be great actually." She said.

Slate smiled taking out a card and pen scribbling something down on it. Then he walked to her side slipping the card into her hand and whispered,

"I'm sure your husband wont mind."

He walked away leaving his fresh scented smell surrounding Brenda in a bubble. She looked down at the card that he had given to her and on it was his cell phone number. She then flipped it over and saw that it was a business card for the C.E.O of the Vega-Rite. Vega-Rite was one of the most famous poker club attractions in the world.

It was a very difficult to get an invite there because they are booked almost every day of the year. And if Slate really did own this place, then that meant he was loaded. It wouldn't even matter if he lost a game of poker or a slot machine beat him, he would have a whole room filled with money to compensate for it. Brenda held the card close to her chest quickly hurrying out of the casino to her car. She looked at the card once more studying the number copying it into her phone book on her cell. She navigated her way straight to her messages about to send Slate a text. But she suddenly stopped once she realized what this text could lead to. It could lead to a friends with benefits relationship, or even worse an affair. But is that what Slate really wanted from her? Or did he just simply want to be friends? She'd been with Terrance, her husband, for over fifteen years. She didn't want it to end because of Slate Stronghouse. After all, he was just a tall and handsome man, only lost once at poker, and is C.E.O of the most popular poker club ever known. But maybe she was just getting in over her head. What if she was just over thinking it and all Slate wanted to be was friends? He did seem like a nice guy so didn't he deserve the benefit of the doubt? Brenda didn't believe he did anything to make her think otherwise. But she figured it was best to wait until tomorrow at least to contact him, she didn't want to seem desperate.

'Another world'

Mika

G inger yawned and woke up with the sun blinding her. She shielded her eyes with her hand moving Drew's arm from around her waist. She slipped on her gray sweatpants and made her way to the bathroom stepping over notebooks, pencils, pens and soda cans.

She stood in front of the mirror and studied herself for a second looking at the fainted bags under her eyes. She pulled on them like she was stretching laffy taffy at a candy shop. Ginger let out a sigh and began to brush her messy hair glancing down at her stomach a couple of times. She heard Drew yawn waking up. He walked into the bathroom hugging Ginger tightly from behind.

"Good morning babe." His voice mumbled against her neck.

Ginger smiled "Good morning." She turned and gave him a soft kiss.

"Sleep well?"

Ginger nodded her head still brushing hair, then slipped a scrunchy off her wrist and tied it into a messy bun.

"We gotta get this place cleaned a little bit because my friends are commin' over." Drew already began to get a head start on picking up some pop cans and placing them in a garbage bag. Ginger began to help by cleaning off the night table.

"Man it was a crazy night wasn't it?" Drew tried to make conversation tying up the garbage bag.

Ginger shrugged, "Yeah I guess so."

"What's wrong?"

"Nothing, I'm just tired I guess." Ginger suddenly felt a wave of nausea. It went into the pit of her stomach and rippled out through the rest of her body like disturbed water, or a line of falling dominoes.

"You ok?" Drew asked walking over to her laying a hand on her shoulder. Ginger looked around, the sun still shining through the shades in her eyes. She bit her lip thinking if she should tell him what was really bothering her. And she thought about it longer than she wanted to, also the response he would give her. And for a moment the wave of nausea seemed to freeze the instant he laid a hand on her bare shoulder, almost like it was also waiting for a response.

"Nothing." Ginger told him shrugging it off. She went into the bathroom quickly closing the door behind her. She leaned against the door sliding down to the floor. It wasn't so much that she needed to vomit, but because she just wanted to separate herself from the rest of the world for a while. Then suddenly she heard knocks on Drew's bedroom door. Ginger figured it was just his friends he had mentioned earlier. She could hear all of them bustling in laughing and talking obnoxiously loud and then she heard one of them say,

"Aye man what's goin' on?"

"Ah you know nothing just been chillin' here for most of the night."

Ginger was thinking about going out there and joining the conversation, but she decided she would rest for a little while longer, just in case the nausea came rushing back to her.

"Hey bro, guess what...look at these pictures this drunk girl took and sent to me."

The conversation began to suddenly get quieter and quieter and a little while later she could hear Drew and his friends outside on the porch talking through the bathroom window.

Drew leaned over anchoring his head down to look and saw a girl with brunette hair in a thong taking off her bra in a modeling tease pose. He put a fist to his mouth and busted out in laughter.

"Wow bro, she must've been like fuckin' wasted. That's just sorda messed up though."

"I know, but she's hot as hell. I'm gonna keep her number and call her when I wanna have a good time."

They both started to laugh almost until they could hardly breathe.

"How old is that chick?" Drew asked.

His friend began to scroll through his phone not answering him for a second, then finally he said,

"She's like...nineteen years old. And she just turned nineteen and she texted me telling me that she wants to make it as a playboy model. And I was like hell yeah send me pictures. She sent me some other ones, one she didn't even have a top on but I can't find 'em."

"Aw that sucks." Drew said leaning over the railing of the porch.

"Haha yeah maybe I should give her your number that way you could have a good time too." They both began to laugh once more. Ginger was eavesdropping on the conversation and her mouth gaped open in disbelief.

"Yeah maybe you should...hahaha nah I'm just kidding."

"So uh, how are you and Ginger doin'?" His friend took a seat in a chair next to Drew.

Drew shrugged, "We're alright."

"Well what's she like? Is she good?"

Drew wheeled around to face him.

"Yeah she's great actually. She's not prude like some of these other chicks."

"Whoa dude, you gotta watch out not to get her pregnant, cuz you know how there are some crazy bitches out there."

"Yeah I know, tell me about it. But even if I did knock her up, I probably wouldn't stay."

Drew's friend laughed. "Seriously dude? You'd leave her?"

"Yeah probably."

Ginger busted out of the bathroom door and came downstairs to meet Drew and his friends on the porch. Drew changed the subject almost instantly.

"So how is school going Matt?"

He shrugged. "I'm failing all my classes dude pretty much. The highest grade I got is a D-. But this one teacher named Ms. Berry; she's such a bitch like no joke."

Drew laughed. "Oh dude, I heard of that teacher too yeah I heard she was a bitch too, I'm glad I didn't have her."

Ginger just sat there watching and listening to the conversation go on. She felt out of place, like a black sheep. She looked down at her stomach, and then up at Drew thinking everything she did was all for him. And now she wished that she had never got involved with him. But it was too late to change her mind.

'Be here now'

Ray LaMontagne

Roy was driving in her car on her way to the station. She was tired and weary and her eyes were dry like cotton.

I knew I should have gotten a coffee at that shop when I had the chance.

Her eyes darted to the clock and she could see that she was running a little late; she sped up the pace. Roy hurriedly turned the corner into a heard of traffic that was barely moving.

Damn I knew I should've taken the back way.

She took a sigh and began to tap her fingers on the steering wheel trying to see around the truck in front of her. To pass up time she turned the radio on and the spokesperson was speaking about the traffic and the weather day forecast. Roy tapped her steering wheel some more wishing the traffic jam would clear. She looked out the window and saw a girl, her back facing traffic, walking to school. She had on a plaid skirt with white knee high socks, black buckled shoes, and a bow in her long blonde wavy hair.

"Morgan?" Roy said to herself. Someone ran up behind the girl and tapped her on the shoulder and Roy could get a clear view of her face once she turned and saw that she wasn't Morgan.

Obnoxious honks made Roy jump and look in the review mirror and saw an angry driver. The driver put up both her hands like she was saying 'Move!' Then a driver pulled up on the side of Roy, rolled down their window and yelled,

"Hey! Why are you just sitting there?! Get the hell out of the way!" And then they sped off further down the street to join the rest of the congestion.

Roy pulled away from the curb, the rain spitting off of her wheels, and took a detour route once she reached an intersection, after all, she was already late as it is.

"Hey where were you?" Jack asked handing her a cup of coffee just a few minutes after she reached her office. She let out a sigh of relief placing her stuff down.

"You would not believe how bad that traffic is out there, it's ridiculous." Roy took a sip of her coffee. "And thanks this is just what I needed."

"No problem, and I know tell me about it. That's why I leave before the traffic jam comes to town." Jack smiled.

Roy smirked opening up a filing cabinet gathering out some yellow notebook paper.

Jack leaned over to get a better look.

"What is that?" He asked nodding his head at the paper.

"Um, just some notes that I scribbled down." Roy's response a little muffled underneath all of the rummaging around of cabinets and papers.

"Jack! Come here please." Their boss yelled and He poked his head out of the doorway and told Roy that he'd be back. Roy gathered all of her notes together in a stack setting them down in front of her at her desk. She flipped through each one reading every word she wrote, and then she laid and spread them apart like a deck of cards to get good view of the overall story each witness said. And yet still, every story was the same until the witness discussed what they had seen Morgan doing that day at practice.

There has to be someone or something else that I'm missing. Roy thought clutching her hair in frustration.

The images of what she witnessed on the CCTV began to train through her mind faster and faster with no caboose. One of Morgan's last moments was imbedded in her mind, all she could see was her frightened expression. And just couldn't begin to imagine what was going through Morgan's mind. But in the midst of all this, she figured she had to back track. Something was telling her that there's something else she's overlooking. Roy threw the notes in the desk drawer, slamming it closed. But then she remembered the diary she had possessed from Morgan's vehicle. Placing the journal on her desk, she let out a deep breath hoping that it would shed some light on the case. Flipping through the pages and skimming Morgan's writing, nothing seemed to stand out. That is until she observed the words, Today is the day I will go. Her eyes squinted and she saw that the entry was created the same day Morgan was last seen. Roy continued to read.

> *Today is the day I will finally get to see Vincent. He's so dreamy I can't get him out of my mind. I don't care what my parents say about him, they'll just have to accept that we are madly in love. I know that meeting someone I met online is risky, but I trust him. Besides, I know he would never hurt me. I'm still having a hard time deciding what to wear. I don't want my mom getting suspicious I know how nosy she can be. I have to make sure that I look perfect for him. He's so sweet. He sent me a necklace in the mail and I will wear it forever. ☺Anyway, off to practice for now.*

Roy didn't see any more writing as she frantically flipped through empty blank pages.

"Well...guess that's all she wrote." Roy said aloud to herself closing the diary feeling optimistic about what she had discovered yet, she was feeling pessimistic that the diary would be able to provide her anything else. Morgan planned to meet a guy named Vincent who she met over the internet. Roy knew now the next step was getting access to Morgan's computer.

"Hey Roy," Jack peeked in getting her attention. "We have copies of the CCTV footage come look." She wasted no time following him to look over the potential evidence.

Jack immediately pressed play on the monitors and the camera was showing a busy intersection. "This was from the hotel a few blocks down, look." He pointed across the street and Morgan could be seen still running and looking behind her from time to time. "The camera only shows a couple frames per second." Jack informed. Morgan was observed hurrying off inside the hotel that the camera was mounted on. Roy, without hesitation, switched to the camera overlooking the lobby.

"Well…why is she still running? I don't see anyone that would be of a threat…" Jack stated.

"She has to be running from something…" Roy answered.

Morgan ran up to the reception desk, which was a little bit out of view, and all that could be seen were her gym shoes. The pair gazed as Morgan darted to the elevators then Roy switched focuses again. The teen frantically pressed the buttons, hastily peeking over her shoulder.

"Who is she looking for? There's no one there." Jack was frustrated.

"I don't know…let's just keep watching…" Roy was scanning the hall once Morgan left to see if there was anyone that looked suspicious or could pose harm.

She kept switching from camera to camera to see where Morgan had gone. The elevators opened and pedestrians got off carrying luggage and other belongings. But Morgan wasn't amongst them.

"Where did she go?" Roy kept converting from one view to another but it was to no avail. The teenager vanished.

"Look at the next floor maybe she went up there." Jack suggested and again, the camera showed an empty hallway.

"Let's scroll back a few seconds earlier while looking at this floor, just to make sure in case we just missed her." The camera, like the other ones, displayed other people exiting; but Morgan wasn't in that crowd either. The pair of detectives were left feeling puzzled.

"So…she's just gone? That's it?" Jack said in shock.

"Yes…I mean you saw it for yourself. She got on the elevator and never came off."

"That's impossible." Jack reached over rewinding the tape and fast forwarding it not believing what his eyes were showing him. "There's no way in hell she just vanished like that. There's no way."

"Well, unless you have another explanation…it sure seems like that."

"No…I know there's something else. There must be another

explanation or something were not looking at. We're going to have to gather the team and watch this again. More eyes on the screen, the more likely we'll get another lead." Jack uttered leaving Roy sitting there intertwined in her thoughts.

"Where did you go Morgan?" She whispered, gaping at the frozen pixels.

She started from the beginning watching frame by frame. Once again, Morgan walks up to the mystery man giving him an embrace. The pair began to walk out of frame and Roy zooms in and notices something she had overlooked. Across the street, a pickup truck transporting scraps and metals, had a mirror mounted amongst the odds and ends that provided a glimpse into the horror occurring in the alleyway. She could barely see it, but the couple stroll down the back way just as a car pulls up. Roy spots a struggle ensue but she can't make out the likeliness of the man or the second person who exits the car. And that's when she sees Morgan emerge staggering down the sidewalk.

"That's why her blouse was torn…" Roy muttered softly her eyes still fixed on Morgan.

She switches the focus to the hotel across the street and that's when she witnesses the car tailing Morgan as she tries desperately to escape from view. The vehicle pulls over in front of the hotel as Morgan rushes in. But the weird thing is, no one gets out to pursue their victim. The car sits there for a little while then abruptly speeds away.

'So low, So high'

Maps

S ophie sat at the table on the pier waiting for Slyder to buy their sandwiches. He came back to the table and laid two baskets down.

"Sorry for taking so long, there was this long line."

Sophie smiled. "It's fine."

They both started eating their sandwich enjoying each other's company.

"So, how's Vermyear? Is it still the same without me?"

Slyder laughed.

"No, it's never gonna be the same without you there. Do you like Cornegy? I heard that place sucks."

Sophie shrugged looking down at her jean shorts. "You're right, it does suck. The people there are rude as hell and there's absolutely no one I mean no one I would ever take the time of day to talk to. Can't wait till I get out of that school.

Slyder smiled and looked off to the roller coaster filled with faint screaming excitement.

"You wanna ride one of the roller coasters with me?" Slyder started to get up throwing away his trash. Sophie finished eating her sandwich and did the same.

"What??? Are you crazy? I hate heights."

Slyder stopped and grabbed her hand.

It'll be fine, just hold on to me if you get scared." He whispered in her ear and then ran down the rest of the pier hand in hand with her. Once they stood in line and took their seats, Sophie's heart beat was taking control of all of her thoughts and feelings until Slyder laced his fingers with her. The coaster started up clicking its way up the hill that was high up it reached the heavens. And once the last click set off and the silence struck. Sophie closed her eyes holding on to Slyder's hand tighter. She opened her eyes from time to time, feeling so low, and then feeling so high. She started screaming louder once she could feel it twisting and turning and she could hear Slyder faintly laugh amongst all of the other screams. She felt the coaster rumble and sway from one direction to another sometimes smooth or rough and jerky other times. Sophie could practically feel her insides become weightless once the coaster reached its highest peak and felt it even more so once it slammed down the slope below. She felt like at any minute she'd fly into the humid air out of her seat. And after the ride came to a close so suddenly, Sophie almost wanted to ride it again. Slyder helped her off the ride making his way through the crowd holding her hand.

"Whoa! That was great, wasn't it?" Slyder smiled holding her around her waist.

Sophie looked down and smiled.

"Yeah it was a little scary at first."

"I know, you held on to me the whole time." He began walking with her down the pier.

"Well you said I could." Sophie couldn't stop smiling being hand in hand with the man of her dreams.

"Ha, maybe tomorrow we can ride another coaster." Slyder picked her up in his arms and carried her to the hotel the rest of the way. She giggled and laughed and held onto him. He carried her up to the hotel room and laid her on the bed.

"So you had a good time?" Slyder asked walking into the bathroom.

Sophie let out a sigh of relief. "Yes, it was fantastic."

Slyder came out of the bathroom hiding something behind his back. "Close you're eyes. I have something for you."

Sophie leaned up on her elbows and closed her eyes. She could feel Slyder sit next to her on the edge of the bed. "Alright, you can open them." He whispered.

Sophie did so, and saw a heart locket with an S engraved on it.

"Oh my gosh Slyder, it's beautiful." Sophie smiled turning allowing Slyder to clasp it around her neck.

"Is that too tight?"

Sophie laid her hand gently on the locket, "No, it's perfect." She turned to him and gave him an embrace. He lifted her up and then let her slide down and they both smiled at each other in silence holding one another.

"I'm glad you like it." Slyder nuzzled her neck and whispered in her ear. Sophie giggled. "I want you to keep it with you always."

"I promise ill take care of it." Sophie laid her hand on the locket again letting this moment and the locket intertwine with her embed in her brain.

'Loosing you'

Late

Sophie was switching her chemistry book with her history one and then slammed the locker door when a pair of hideous argyle socks filled her peripheral vision. Sophie gave a dirty look.

"Hey Sophs."

Sophie began to walk away from her down the crowded hallway and Marribell hurriedly followed behind.

"I told you stop calling me that." Sophie rolled her eyes hugging her books close to her chest.

Marribell clasped her hand over her mouth. "Oopsies! Sorry my bad." "Oh hey by the way there's this little party tonight wanna go?"

Sophie shook her head. "Sorry but I'm not interested."

Marribell skipped in front of Sophie in her obnoxious polka dotted rain boots cutting her off.

"Could you get out of my way?" Sophie snarled.

Marribell's eyes locked on Sophie's silver shiny chain wrapped around her neck.

"OOOOOO! What's that 'S' stand for in the heart?" Marribell's pointed finger followed Sophie going around her.

Marribell's eyes squinted following Sophie behind.

"Wait a second…that's not from Slyder is it? I told you to stay away from him." Marribell became serious but Sophie laughed like she told a funny joke.

"Relax Marribell I'm not serious with him yet."

"Yet?? You should never get serious with him ever. If you do then you're stupid."

Sophie simply just ignored her walking into her classroom thinking that she couldn't believe Marribell had the nerve to call her stupid when she's the one wearing clown outfits.

"Well at least think about the party tonight Sophs!" Marribell yelled from out in the hallway waving her hand like she was waving fair well off to a solider going in for battle.

Sophie truly wasn't sure if she wanted to go to the party. Not only because her and Slyder were thinking about hanging out tonight, but because she didn't want to show up with Marribell as her date. But the more she thought about it, she was hanging out with Slyder a little too much and not Marribell anymore. But regardless, Sophie needed to get away from her for a while but then again, Slyder and she could always hang out a different day. With that in mind Sophie slowly snuck out her phone glancing around to make sure the teacher wasn't anywhere near by and sent him a text saying:

We can't hang out tonight.

Thinking he'd be understanding and just go along with it she dumped her phone back in her coach purse when she felt a vibration seconds later against the side of her shoe. She grabbed her bag and placed it on her lap looking at the text that read:

And why is that?

Sophie sat there thinking weather or not to tell him she had plans with someone else or just lie to him. But before she could move her thumb to begin typing her phone vibrated again with another text from him.

Well whatever it is it's not a good excuse.

Sophie sank in her chair like a sinking ship covering up her phone while the teacher walked by over to her desk setting down a stack of papers. Sophie kept looking up at the teacher and quickly looking back down at her phone.

We'll just hang out a different day.

Sophie received another text from him seconds later.

Ok...whatever.

She texted him back quickly.

I have to go now.

"Textinginclass." Someone coughed a few seats behind Sophie. She turned around and the guy who said it gave a friendly smile and wave. Sophie turned back around dropping her bag on the floor. For the rest of class she could feel her purse vibrate against her shoe and the desk but she ignored it. During passing period, Sophie quickly made her way to the girls' bathroom pulling out her phone and saw she had a few messages but was disappointed when she saw the messages were just from her mother. She rolled her eyes and dunked her phone in her purse and walked out but stopped once she heard faint yells coming from around the corner

"FIGHT! FIGHT! FIGHT!" Sophie heard a crowd of people yelling and she followed the sound like Dorothy going down the yellow brick road and came across a whole mob of students surrounding two people. Some of them had their hands in the air like they were at a concert and others were on their tippy toes grabbing onto the shoulders of other kids trying to get a good view. Sophie quickly came at the crowd preparing herself to be thrown around by students' arms and bodies pushing her way through and reached a tiny open spot to get a good view of what the commotion was all about. She saw two boys she didn't recognize walking slowly in circles like vultures looking for prey. One boy came at the other and slammed him against the lockers like an angry bull and began to punch him in the pit of his stomach, the crowd around Sophie began to scream with excitement.

"COME ON KICK HIS ASS!" Sophie heard a guy from the crowd yell cupping his hands around his mouth. Sophie saw Ms. Hendrick, her chemistry teacher, weaving her way through the out of control crowd slightly staggering over to the boys, her tan button down top was slightly undone and Sophie didn't know weather it was because she was fighting the crowd or she was too busty to fit her top. She grabbed one of the boys by his collar and the other by the back of his tight fitted shirt and the crowd quieted down.

"Everyone go to class!" She turned her attention back to the two boys in her tight grasp.

"And you two...go to the office." She said giving them a little push to send them on their way.

The once out of control mob surrounding Sophie tightly had dwindled down to ten students but soon they dissolved into the groups who were departing. The two boys walked away with their heads down still looking steamed. Ms. Hendrick gave a warm smile breathing heavily with her hands on her slim hips.

She looked down at her top and quickly began to button it back up.

"I think you should um…head to class Sophie before you're late." She gestured down the hallway pulling down her bunched up scarlet skirt and straightened it out.

Sophie gave a smirk and nodded leaving going to her next class. Ms. Hendricks straightened out her blouse glancing around her to make certain there were no other students. She walked back into her classroom and observed Entino by the open window taking a drag of his cigarette airing it out wedged in the window pane. She smirked and walked over joining him at his side. She rested her face against his shoulder embracing him from behind.

"I'm so happy with you Entino." She spoke smiling once more. But her smile vanished a bit once she noticed his response was silence. "Are you happy with me?"

Entino just shrugged continuing to smoke. Ms. Hendricks spun him around.

"What's that supposed to mean?"

"It means I don't know." He started to turn back to the window when Ms. Hendricks forced him to face her again.

"How do you not know if you're happy with someone you've been with for the past year?" She demanded an answer.

"Look…Beth…you knew what this was from the beginning. What did you expect?"

"What did I expect? I expected for us to be together forever." Ms. Hendricks started to get upset, her voice began to tremble. Entino just stood there looking her in the eyes so intently it almost felt like he was trying to hypnotize her. "Don't you look at me like that." She commanded. And Entino finished his cigarette flicking it out the window proceeding to brush passed her. "You have nothing to say to me?"

"What do you want me to say?"

"I want you to say that you love me and want to be with me."

Entino smirked. "Heh, oh Beth…you're so pathetic… so useless." He continued to the door to leave.

"That's not what you were telling me last night is it?" She spat edging over to him. He sighed and turned to face her. "You were telling me how much you loved me…how much you wanted to be with me… do you remember that?"

Entino folded his arms and didn't seem like he wanted to give an answer or even be bothered by her presence.

"Is there someone else?" She asked standing face to face with him. Entino gave a devilish smirk. "Who is it?... tell me!" Ms. Hendrick shouted ordering him to comply.

"You may want to keep your voice down…wouldn't want to disturb study hall next door." He answered passive aggressively.

She rushed to him raising her hand to slap him but Entino didn't even flinch a muscle. He remained calm and collect supported against the door. "Do it…hit me." He encouraged her leaning in closer to her hand. "Go ahead…right here. Do it." He smiled. Ms. Hendrick lowered her hand shaking her head moving away from him. "Just like I said, pathetic and useless." He walked to where she sat at her desk and he leaned over, placing his hands down for support so she could see him square in the eyes. "No wonder why your husband hates you."

"You don't know anything about my marriage. So, leave my husband out of this."

"I know that you weren't happy. And you still aren't. Otherwise… we wouldn't be here…with you being so sad…so pitiful…" Ms. Hendricks baby blue eyes began to swell up with tears.

"It's all your fault…you gave me false hope…you made me believe you really loved me. But I promise you…I will find out who the other woman is."

"Heh…" He began shaking his head in disgust. "You couldn't even if you tried. You're not that smart Beth."

"That's what you think…"

Entino rolled his eyes proceeding to leave again. "I don't have time for this…besides I have homework to do."

"Trust me…I won't let you go. You'll always be mine Entino

Awuz. I'll never stop loving you…or wanting you. I would kill for you if I had to."

His back was facing her as he paused at the door. He turned his head and she could only be seen in his peripheral vision.

"Beth…you're such a victim."

"I know I am." She agreed a burning rage boiling in her from within.

"A victim of your own stupidity." He finally walked out slamming the door in her face. The sound of the door being shut caused Ms. Hendrick to break down completely. The tears streamed down her face as she gasped for air laying back in her chair. She yanked some tissues out wiping her eyes trying her best to calm down and catch her breath. When she saw the door slam, he closed the door to her feelings. And slammed the door on their relationship. But Ms. Hendrick was scorned and she meant exactly what she promised to him. She wasn't going to loosen her grip that easily vowing that nothing or anyone would get in her way.

Once the final bell rang for school to end Sophie was one of the first students out of the building turning up the volume of her phone. She took a deep breath happily making her way to the bus glad the day was over casually walking down the pavement.

"Hey Soph!" Sophie heard an annoying familiar voice and turned around.

Damn.

"Man you walk so fast." Marribell said panting her words out leaning over with her hands on her bony knees.

"I know… it gets you places faster you should try it sometime."

Sophie and Marribell began walking together.

"So uh…have you thought about the party yet? Are you going??" Marribell squealed walking side ways to keep up with Sophie's quick steps.

Sophie shrugged.

"Well depends…who's throwing this little party?"

"Reg."

Sophie stopped and gave a confused stare.

"Who?"

"Reg. That's her nick name, her real name is Regan but she doesn't like when people call her that." Marribell explained.

"Fine…I'll go. BUT…don't embarrass me. If you in anyway act stupid I'm hightailing the hell out of there." Sophie warned.

Marribell nodded her head in agreement her bangs dangling in front of her eyes like a theater curtain.

"Okie dokie artichokie! I promise you it'll be fun!" Marribell skipped off forcing a couple to separate from holding hands. The couple gave dirty stares as she darted past them.

"That's exactly what I was talking about." Sophie mumbled under breath getting on her bus and once she arrived home she heard her cell phone start to ring as soon as she walked through the door. Sophie looked at her phone and saw it was Marribell.

"Hello?" Sophie said

"Hey lemon drop! Be ready when I get there I'm comin' down the road to getcha!"

"What? Why are you coming over here for?" Sophie sounded annoyed.

"Well we have to go get our costumes duh! It's a Halloween party dontcha know? Be ready when I get there I can't talk and drive! Toodles!" Marribell hung up on Sophie and she rolled her eyes. And not even a second later, she heard an obnoxious horn outside of her window. Sophie looked out through the shades and saw Marribell in huge yellow sunglasses waving from the car window. Sophie came out of the house and hops in Marribell's car. "Don't forget your seat belt cookie. Safety first!"

Sophie rolled her eyes again putting her hand on her head looking out of the window.

"Ok so I know this fantastic place we can go to to get costumes. It's this place called Halloween Galore. I love it. I go there almost every year to get Halloween decorations. It's gonna be amazing!" Marribell squealed.

"Yeah…sure…whatever…" Sophie said plainly wishing she chose to hang out with Slyder instead. Marribell pulled into a parking spot cutting someone off. The person honked loudly and yelled obscenities out of the window.

"Geeze, I guess that person isn't having a good day." Marribell said looking at herself in the mirror and then hoping out. "Ok let's go!" Marribell hurried out of the car dangling Sophie by one arm. And they were greeted with scream saying his famous line, "Whazzzuppp?!!"

"Isn't this place cool?" Marribell said excitedly almost getting hit with flying toy bats.

"Yeah…" Sophie began looking at a life size tarantula on the floor. "Sure is."

"Hi!" A girl who worked there greeted them dressed like a fantasy fairy. "Welcome to Halloween Galore, our costumes are buy one get one half off and of course if you're a member of our store you get a third one for free! My name is Stacy if you need anything." Stacy gave a wide grin with sparkles on her skin glistening and hurried off to meet other customers.

"Thanks Stacy!" Marribell yelled after her. "Gosh I love that girl, she's so nice. She's here almost every year when I come here to get stuff." Marribell stopped in one of the aisles and kneeled down getting a better look at the costumes. "Hmm…what do you think Soph? Which one should we get?"

Sophie looked at the rack of costumes and saw her options:

One she could be Shrek. Two she could be a sugarplum fairy. Or three she could be a sexy nurse. *Yeah I'm not looking like Shrek or a dumb fairy or even a slut for Halloween.*

Sophie turned around and looked at the other side and saw cat ears and a tail.

"This'll do. Lets go." She said plainly grabbing the cat ears and tail off of the shelf.

"But…but…Sophie…" Marribell followed her. "But what about my costume?"

"I don't care what you get." Sophie stood in the long line to pay.

"But you have to help me find one I helped find yours." Marribell wined.

"Sure."

Marribell ignored her and dragged her by one arm again down another aisle with screaming kids and their parents not paying any attention to them.

"OOOOO!" Marribell screamed which made the winy kids shut up and stare.

"What is your problem?" Sophie grabbed her arm and spoke through her teeth.

"I wanna get this costume, this looks cool." Marribell grabbed a pumpkin costume from the rack. "I'll get this." She said placing the costume bag over her body posing in the mirror.

"Ok…um…let's go…" Sophie said walking off embarrassed. And she was even more embarrassed once they got to Marribell's house and put their costumes on. Sophie looked at Marribell's costume and the pumpkin looked more swollen than it did on the bag.

"What's…wrong with it…?" Sophie asked staring at her through the mirror almost speechless.

Marribell turned to face her. "What do you mean what's wrong with it? Don't you think it's cool?" She posed in it.

"Um…no…it's just a lot going on…you have the green tights that are too loose, and then you have the pumpkin top hat."

Marribell shrugged. "What's wrong with that?"

"But why are you so swollen looking? You're supposed to look like this." Sophie held up the bag with a picture of a girl with the costume on only the pumpkin looked slimmer.

"Well I stuffed it with newspaper."

"You what?"

"Yeah I thought it looked kind of boring all flat and stuff so I just took some newspaper and stuffed it."

"That's kiddie stuff…that's what kindergartners do." Sophie spat but she knew it wouldn't put an end to Marribell's craziness.

"Well let's see your costume." Marribell ignored her. Sophie got her cat ears from off the bed and put them on her head and stood up showing her tail she tied around herself. "What are you suppose to be?" Marribell asked confused.

"I'm an alley cat….meow.." Sophie said plainly.

"Hmmm…interesting…Well let's go! We don't wanna be late for the party." Marribell squealed rushing down the stairs.

"Ok listen Marribell it's not cool to be the first one to show up at a party especially if you look like that. And how are you gonna fit in your car?" Sophie got in waiting for Marribell to squeeze herself.

"I'll...manage..." Marribell grunted finally plopping into the driver seat, her belly almost touching the steering wheel. And she almost ran over everything the whole ride there and once they arrived Sophie stopped her before she could get out of the car.

"Now listen to me..." Sophie said sternly. "If you embarrass me... in any way and I mean any kind of way. I'm leaving and you're taking me home as soon as possible. Got it?"

Marribell nodded her head with her pumpkin hat bobbing up and down. They both got out of the car and walked up to the house and saw some guys shirtless drinking beer and teepying the house. And a couple making out by the front door and Sophie and Marribell walked into low music and smokers at almost every corner of the house. Sophie observed people making out on the couch and couples grouping each other and dark lonely corners.

"Wooo! This is fun." Marribell said aloud and started doing the robot. Sophie stopped her and grabbed her arm.

"What did I say Marribell?"

"Well then let's dance together!" Marribell squealed following Sophie down the hall. Sophie zoned her out and kept walking. She needed to get away from her and the smokers because she couldn't stand either one of them. Sophie opened a door and walked in closing it behind her taking a deep breath. She turned around leaning on the door and closed her eyes for a moment and then opened them. Her legs became paralyzed and her heart followed. She saw Entino Auwz dressed as a matador wiping something off of his loose fitted shirt. And he looked up at her and her eyes were fixed on yellow. Sophie began to bite her lip and felt like she was gasping for oxygen. *Oh my gosh...he's so hot..*

He looked down again and his hair covered his face.

"It's occupied." He calmly stated.

"Well the door wasn't locked." Sophie responded carelessly looking at herself in the mirror fixing her cat ears. Entino moved toward her.

"I said...it's fucking occupied."

Sophie gave him a dirty look glaring him up and down. "I said the door wasn't fucking locked." She stared at him in his bright yellowish eyes. He studied her and he suddenly began to move towards her. Entino backed her up to the door and the air became still as Sophie. They stared intently at each other. Sophie's breaths were broken and she felt Entino's hand move behind her locking the bathroom door. The sound of the latch clicking down echoed throughout the silent air, like it was a signal for something to happen. He moved his hand over her shirt up to her neck and face and Sophie started to push him away but he was too strong. She raised her hand to hit him but Entino grabbed her arm ever so swiftly, kissing it all the way up to her hand. Sophie closed her eyes and turned her head away.

He took her hand and laced fingers pressing her against the door leaning in tenderly kissing her neck. His lip piercing was digging into her skin now and again. She kept trying to push him away but the touch of his lips, so tender and passionate, surpassed her feeling of wanting him to stop. He continued to kiss her neck the flesh of his lips brushing on her skin after each consecutive touch. *Oh my gosh what am I doing? How could I do this behind Slyder's back? After everything he's done for me? How could I go behind his back and do this? But oh gosh he feels so good grinding against me I don't know if I can stop. Why didn't I just leave the bathroom when I had the chance? But he makes me feel so good I can't stop now.* She thought to herself. Sophie loved his painful pleasure.

Her fingers went through his dark slick hair, clenching on to his shirt and his kisses became more prominent, hard, and forceful.

"Hmm…Entino…don't stop…" Sophie uttered moaning through breaths in his ear burrowing her finger nails into his skin. He stopped and looked at her in her eyes. He guided his hand up to her lips his thumb rubbed softly across them and Sophie shuddered at his touch. He suddenly bent down slightly pulling her thighs around him raising her up in his strong powerful arms.

Right away Sophie started to kiss him hard pulling him closer to her. Entino did the same placing her gently on the counter. His hand glided along her thigh and up her shirt over her chest causing Sophie to moan gently through their rough eager kisses. Entino began to grind against her yanking her hips down and out to him. He wanted to have his way with her. Allowing herself to be vulnerable to his needs and desires, she laid back on the sink creating hand prints on the mirrors. He kept shoving his hips forward pulling her to him with every moan Sophie cried out. She put her head back biting her lip feeling the weight of Entino's tight body lean over her the thrusts becoming more firm and direct. Sophie never expected she could receive such fulfillment and pleasure from dry sex. He knew all of her weak spots, all the parts that longed for his touch, his caress and it drove her insane. Entino gave every part of her body the attention it wanted. He kissed her neck and moved up to her lips kissing her sensually. He pulled her up off the counter letting her slide till her feet touched the floor. Sophie's hand stroked over his stomach, his chest, and she leaned in kissing his neck delicately letting herself to succumb to him as she got sucked in closer and closer. He leaned in again and began kissing her obsessively, directing her over to the wall pushing her against it. Sophie wrapped her arms around his neck and for a moment the pleasure stopped and they stared into each other's eyes which were bursting with sensual upmost satisfaction. Nothing but heavy breathing filled the silence. Entino started kissing her once more, her hand fell between them and without even really thinking rested on his bulging package. Sophie slightly jumped when she felt how large and pleased it became in the palm of her hand, feeling she didn't have control in that moment of her body, feelings, or movements. Her body started to undergo an outer body experience. Suddenly there was a knock at the door that startled them both.

"Shit." Sophie said quickly unlocking the door stepping out into the hall. Entino made sure he wasn't seen. Sophie saw Marribell coming towards her and she placed her hand on her head.

"Hey there squirt!" Marribell yelled running down the hall in her embarrassing costume. "Woo that's some party over there. I did way too much runnin' around. I gotta use the loo, excuse me." Marribell stated about to grab the door knob until Sophie stopped her.

"Don't go in there!"

"But why n-

The door opened cutting her off and Entino stepped out zipping his pants up looking Sophie straight in the eye. And she gave him a glare of unbelief. They both watched him walk away down the hall mixing into the wasted crowd.

"Well it's free now! Oh and by the way your lips are bleeding." Marribell yelled licking her thumb and pressed it against Sophie's forehead. Sophie could see the buttoned flap in the back of Marribell's swollen costume as she slammed the door behind her. Sophie rubbed her fingers against her lip and saw a smudge of red. She slid down to the floor not wanting to be at this party thinking about the intimate moment between her and Entino. The last kiss he gave her spoke to her through his soft hurtful lips. It told her to remember how he pleasured her and take it home. She placed her fingers over her lips where Entino had made her bleed. And later that night, Sophie lay in bed thinking of the moment she shared with Entino as she stared at the ceiling, barely even blinking. She reached around her neck about to take off her locket necklace when she didn't feel it there. Sophie immediately sat up and looked on her night stand to see if she'd forgot she took it off but it wasn't there. She looked under her pillow next and then on the floor. The locket was the only thing keeping her and Slyder together when they were apart, and now it was gone.

'Something'

Jmsn

Ginger got out of the shower grabbing a towel ringing out her dripping wet hair. She wiped away the steam from the mirror studying her nude body up and down from right to left. She stood back from the mirror and assessed herself from the side. She knew that her stomach wouldn't have a bump yet, but she just couldn't help but think there's something there inside of her and that won't go away until a while. She heard a knock on the door and before Ginger could compose herself, the door opened allowing the icy air to rush in. Ginger covered up her body quickly with a towel and Drew smiled.

"Geeze Drew you could've warned me you were coming in or something."

"I did...I knocked." Drew laughed a little and grabbed Ginger from behind feeling the wet warmth of her body. He began to gently kiss her neck opening up the towel from around her. Ginger shivered a little turning around to face him. She began to kiss him soft and gently wrapping her arms around his neck. He pushed her up against the sink as his hand trailed down between her damp creamy thighs and she stopped him moving away.

"Babe what's wrong?" Drew followed her out of the bathroom.

"It's just...I'm not in the mood right now."

"You're never in the mood anymore. Did I do something wrong?"

Ginger turned to look at him straight in his brown eyes. She lowered her eyes to the floor. "No...things just don't feel the same."

Drew laughed to himself sitting at his computer desk. "Well things are only what you make them."

"Look Drew I just have a lot of things going on right now ok? I just...-

"I mean you used to be in the mood all the time. We used to shut the lights off and fuck around. Now you're just.... boring."

Ginger turned to face the back of his head while he continued to type on his computer.

"What? I'm boring? I'm boring because I don't wanna fuck you all the time?"

Drew spun around in his chair to face her. "Noo...you're boring because you don't wanna do anything at all all the time. Ever. I mean Jesus Christ Ginger surely you can't be on your monthly this long."

"Oh you go to hell." Ginger said to him slipping on her underwear and bra.

Drew went up to her grabbing her arm tightly yanking and forcing her to face him. "Seriously Ginger what the fuck is wrong with you?"

She jerked her arm away. "Nothing. I'm boring remember?" Ginger walked away from him looking for some clothes to put on.

"Tell me what is wrong. Did I do something? Did your mother do something? Family drama? You're pregnant? what?"

Ginger looked at him. At first, she was thinking now was her chance. But she just couldn't bring herself to tell him now. She wanted to wait a little longer even though she knew later on down the line she'd regret it. But she didn't care. She was being selfish toward her future self because right now Drew was pissing her off.

"You didn't do anything...my mother didn't do anything...and there's no family drama...and no...I'm not pregnant..."

"Good." Drew sat back down at his computer desk.

"...But what if I was?" Ginger quietly asked.

Drew shrugged. "Well then...I guess we would just take care of it."

"Oh, so you'd stay?"

Drew shrugged taking a chug of his soda. "I don't know...I just don't think I'd be ready for any of that responsibility. You said you were on the pill anyway so we have nothing to worry about."

"Maybe you don't have anything to worry about but I do."

"Oh my gosh Ginger I'm not in the mood for this right now." He twirled back around putting his head phones on and Ginger marched over and snatched them off his head.

"Ow! What the hell was that for?" Drew bellowed looking up at her.

"Because I'm trying to talk to you about something and you put your head phones on and ignored me."

He rolled his eyes. "There's nothing to talk about." He continued to spin around about to put his head phones on again when Ginger jerked them off again and he let out a long sigh standing up. "You know what I'm gonna go for a drive I'll be back."

"Wait where are you going?"

"Out...don't wait up." He slammed the door leaving Ginger standing there and she shook her head feeling tears rising. She turned her attention over to the computer and decided to snoop.

She opened the tab and was happy to see he left his pixal me account open. Ginger clicked the messages and immediately saw numerous messages from different girls. All of them she read were just casual conversation and she was about to exit but something caught her eye. She squinted into the screen and clicked on one of the messages and witnessed nude pictures of a girl she didn't recognize. Ginger was disgusted as she kept scrolling through them and saw she had a tramp stamp of a pink heart. She scrolled down and saw Drew responded with: You never fail to impress me ;)

She messaged him back: It's all for you babe xoxoxo ;)

Ginger slammed the laptop down her mouth hanging open in disbelief. She never experienced this much betrayal in her life, this much pain. Now she knew if she did tell him about her secret he would likely leave her for sure.

Chapter Twenty-Two

"This is a very nice place. And thanks again for meeting us for dinner." Brenda said with a cheesy smile sliding down in the booth and Terrance slid in next to her.

Slate gave a white bright smile. "Hey it's no problem. Besides I love to wine and dine."

"Yeah do you do this with a lot of married couples? Just…wine and dine them both?" Terrance said matter of factly. Brenda discreetly squeezed his thigh letting him know where his boundaries lie. Slate chuckled opening the menu.

"Only the ones I like." Slate glanced at Brenda and she smiled back at him shyly. The piano playing and chatter in the background helped fill the awkward silence at the table.

"So…Slate." Terrance began. "What is it that you do?" He leaned forward on the table.

"Well." Slate flipped a page in the menu. "I'm an entrepreneur." Slate smiled that bright charming smile.

"Of what?"

"Well I'm the C.E.O of the most popular casino joint in the nation. The Vega-Rite. Ever heard of it?" He placed down his menu. Terrance eyes were slits. He looked Slate up and down a hill against a mountain.

"You've heard of it haven't you dear?" Brenda said disturbing his thoughts.

"Yeah…of course I've heard of it."

"Thought so." Slate said. "Um waiter…we're ready to order." Slate snapped his fingers and the waiter promptly waited on them.

"So…Terrance…" Slate began leaning in closer eye to eye with him. "What is it that you do?"

"I'm a chef." He retorted.

"Hmm…I see…that's fantastic actually because I was seeking a new chef. The one I have now is on the verge of... retiring."

"Thanks but no thanks." Terrance refused folding his arms.

"Well how much would I have to pay you to come work for me?"

"More than you could ever afford."

Slate chuckled taking a sip of his wine. "Everyone and everything has a price Terrance...anything can be bought..." Slate said mysteriously staring him down

"My answer is still and will always be no."

"Ok...fine...fair enough." Slate gave a sinister smile relaxing back in his chair. Terrance yawned obnoxiously.

For the rest of the dinner it was mostly Brenda and Slate talking with Terrance mostly smiling, nodding, and staring down Slate. After the agonizing dinner, Brenda thanked him again giving him a hug while Terrance stood there awkwardly. He shook hands with Slate and watched him walk into the dead of night.

"Drive safe!" Brenda yelled after him. Terrance rolled his eyes getting in the car with Brenda.

"Wasn't that a lovely dinner?" Brenda said putting her seat belt on.

"Yeah...just fantastic." He said in a monotone voice yanking his seat belt on and quickly driving off.

"What's wrong?"

"Nothing absolutely nothing." Terrance said also in monotone.

"What you didn't enjoy the dinner?" Brenda asked.

"Yeah I did. I would have enjoyed it even more if it was just the two of us."

"Oh, so that's what this is about? You didn't want Slate to come?"

"No fuckin' duh."

Brenda looked shocked.

"Ok first of all, he invited us to dinner with him. And he paid the bill plus the tip."

"Oh, yeah what the fuck was that about? The bill comes he snatches it up holding the bill hostage like I don't have a job to pay for it?" Terrance said irritated.

"He was just being nice. How dare you say that." Brenda defended him.

"Oh, you're right how dare I. How dare I say the truth. It could've been just me and you but no you had to go out with mother fucking jack pot jones."

"Oh my gosh you are so unbelievable. You know what at least he actually takes me out you don't do shit for me anymore."

Terrance slammed on his brakes making Brenda jerk forward causing a whip lash. She grabbed her neck wincing. "Gosh Terrance what the hell is your problem?"

"What's my problem? What's my problem? You know what you can spread your venomous disease of an attitude all you want because I didn't sign up for this shit."

Brenda shook her head in disbelief looking out the window. "You know what Terrance just take me home."

"Gladly." Terrance sped off into the night.

"You really are an asshole sometimes you know that?"

"Ok I'm sorry."

Brenda raised her eyebrows astonished by the admission of guilt. "Apology accepted."

"Yeah, I'm sorry that I wasn't okay with some random, rude, rich guy, wine and dine you and I. And for making me feel like less than a man, and for trying to set some boundaries, and sorry I couldn't be Mr. Money Bags for you, and FOR TAKING YOU TO THIS STUPID DAMN DINNER TO BEGIN WITH!" Terrance's voice released a powerful bellow.

"Oh please, don't blame me for your insecurities."

"Insecurities? I'm insecure because I don't want another man flirting with my wife?"

"We were just talking and having a conversation, that's it." Brenda assured. "And I think you should take him up on his offer."

"What offer?" Terrance glanced over his eyebrows raised.

"Of going to work for h-."

"Nope absolutely not going to happen. I'd never want to work for that prick regardless if it was the last job on earth. I'd rather work for satin."

"But think about it though, this would really be good for us. It would help with some of the bills and maybe we can pay off the house and go out on a vacation. Doesn't that sound great?"

"Of course, it does but…it's not going to happen. Why don't you go work for him? I mean you guys are already comfortable around each other. Plus, you'll have an excuse to go see him."

"Terrance I'm not in the mood to argue. All I'm saying is you should consider it."

The next morning, Terrance was on his way to work still irritated about last night. He wasn't sure exactly what Slate's motives were, but he knew that it didn't involve anything good. He couldn't quite figure out why but every time he was around he felt very uneasy. Terrance was scared for himself and his wife. She seemed to be too far gone into his spell that she passed the point of no return and that bothered him. He pulled into the parking lot of his work and was surprised there was plenty of spots available.

"Hmm…that's weird…it's close to lunch time we're usually flooded with people by now." He observed quietly to himself. He parked and glanced at his surroundings to see if he saw any of his regulars but it was just silent and bare. He shrugged and got out walking up to the doors and was startled with confusion when they were locked.

"What?…why is this locked? Today's not a holiday…" Terrance suddenly noticed on a sign on the door that read 'under new management. Beau Cannon industries.'

'We do what we want to'

O+S

Later on that day, Roy was ending her shift gathering her things and her purse. She was about to leave when one of her coworkers Amy appeared suddenly in the doorway. Roy was startled.

"Oh! You scared me." Roy laughed it off and Amy did the same.

"Sorry I didn't mean to."

"Its ok, so what did you need?"

"Oh well me and some coworkers were gonna go out for some drinks you wanna come?"

"Oh well...sure...and it's the lounge right? Not far from here?"

"Yeah same as always." Amy laughed already walking away to gathering her belongings.

"Alright I'll meet you guys there." Roy said making her way to her car. She followed the rest of her coworkers and was coming out into the intersection looking both ways when all of the sudden a sleek black Lamborghini sped down the street hitting the front left side of her pink Slug Bug. Roy immediately slammed on her brakes spinning out of control her tires screeching on the pavement but it was of no use since the damage was already done. Everything in the back of her car came flying into the passenger side and both of her shoes came right off sliding underneath the brake pedal. Roy's mouth was gawked open from shock and once she got all of her red hair from in front of her face she peered out of her review mirror saw the owner of the Lamborghini rushing over seeming concerned.

"I'm so sorry ma'am are you alright?" Roy faintly heard the man say. She was barely paying attention due to the ringing in her ears. She was pissed off because not only was he speeding he didn't even stop when he saw her coming out into the intersection. She got out of the car straightening out her black pants suit and fixing her hair.

"Did you not look where the fuck you were going?!" Roy slightly raised her voice until she realized that the man, even though he caused an accident, was very easy on the eyes.

"I know ma'am I'm so sorry I was just late for an appointment so that's why I was rushing. But are you ok?"

"Yeah I'm fine but we have to exchange insurance information and contact information and then-."

"How much was your car?" The man suddenly asked.

Roy looked confused. "Why?"

"Just tell me how much was it? $6,000? Maybe $7,000?"

"It was actually $8,000."

"Oh really? Well here how about this." He began pulling his check book from out of his back pocket. "I'll write you a check for $10,000. You can use the $8,000 to buy a new car and the other $2,000 to treat yourself to something for the inconvenience." He finished writing and ripped the check from out of his check book handing it over to her with his charming smile. Roy blinked with amazement, speechless, wondering what kind of job does he have that he would have all this money.

"Thank you but...I can't take that you can just pay what the damages are worth it's not necessary." Roy insisted feeling guilty that she shouted.

"Do I have to hunt you down and deposit it myself?" The man offered once more. Roy looked at him with shocked uneasy eyes, and then looked at the check in his hand. She was contemplating, wondering if she really should just take the money. She just thought he'd have the insurance pay for the damages, not him paying for the cost of the whole car. But then she thought why not take advantage of this?

"Well actually," Roy took the check willingly out of his hand and began looking at the front of her car where the impact occurred,

"Looking at these damages and stuff I think it's actually worth $15,000."

The man laughed. "And how do you figure?"

"$10,000 for the damages, and $15,000 for my time." Roy crossed her arms looking entitled. The man laughed slicking his hair back.

" Heh cute."

Roy wasn't impressed her eyes narrowed. The man took out his check book from out of his back pocket again. "Well here's ANOTHER check for $15,000 so now you can go buy yourself a brand new car and treat yourself to something nice." He ripped it out of his check book and before he could even hand it over Roy snatched it from out of his hand.

"Who are you?" Roy questioned somewhat intrigued.

"Oh my apologies I didn't introduce myself, my name is Carter Lincoln BeaCannon." He smiled and Roy gave a sneer.

"Well I'm gonna need your information so I can find you when these checks bounce." The man laughed putting his check book away.

"You're a real piece of work aren't you lady?" She turned around to face him with a dirty look.

"Well...I was wondering if I could treat you to dinner tonight or maybe this weekend. Wait where are you going?"

The man laughed once more following Roy to her car.

"I'm going to call a tow truck because that's how it looks like I'm getting home now."

"Well you don't have to worry about that my buddy owns one not far from here so I'm sure he wouldn't mind towing your car." He took out his cell phone and called. And Roy rolled her eyes getting in the driver side of her car crossing her arms. The man came up to her driver side window and Roy rolled it down.

"What do you want?" She asked.

"I was just telling you that I called and they're on the way so... they should be here in about 10 minutes." The man said looking at his watch.

"Ok thanks." Roy began rolling up the window when the man stopped her.

"Wait...do you think I can give you a call sometime?" The man gave her a warm charming smile and even though Roy loved his physique, his dark brown leather hair, his closely shaven beard, and his scent was intoxicating, but nonetheless she still wasn't impressed.

"My number's in the phone book." She started rolling up her window more and he stopped her again.

"Well wait what's your name so I can find you." He smiled again.

"You'll find that in the book too." Roy rolled up the window all the way and she saw the man smile and shake his head. He placed his hands in his suit pockets walking back to his car whistling a tune. He got back in his car and rolled down the window that way he was making eye contact with Roy. She tried not to look at him but it was hard not to since he was right there in front of her. He smiled and the tow truck pulled up behind him. The man winked at Roy and drove off and her eyes locked on him following his car down the street until she couldn't see him anymore.

The next evening Roy was sitting at her desk with the Morgan Stasney case file sprawled out like a deck of cards. She looked and studied everything that they have gathered so far. Roy picked up a photo from out of the file of Morgan and studied it closely. Morgan looked so happy in her cheerleading uniform posing with her pom-poms and Roy often wondered, when they get missing persons' cases, how they could look so happy and so nice and then the next minute vanish. Roy hung her head, her red hair covering her face, trying her best to think of where to look next. Suddenly the door swung open and she saw Jack walk in with a pink Dell laptop setting it down on Roy's desk. She scrunched her face up confused. "What's this?"

"Well do you want the good news or the bad news?" Jack asked shoving is hands in his pockets. Roy let out a sigh folding her arms.

"Fine what's the good news?"

"The good news is this is Morgan's laptop." Jack answered giving a half smile. Roy let out a laugh.

"Ok…so…what is the bad news?"

"The bad news is we need the charger and can't locate it."

Roy sighed, "That's just terrific…how did you even get into her house and get this?"

"I didn't. This was found in the woods."

"In the woods?"

"Yeah I know...I have no idea how it got there. And not far from this a backpack was found along the stream."

"Was there anything in it?"

"Yes, it was Morgan's cheerleading outfit and her socks and her shoes."

"Hmm..." Roy got the diary out and flipped to the last entry that was made. "She said that she was having a hard time deciding what to wear. And that...she didn't want her mother getting suspicious. So, if she was wearing her cheerleading outfit when she was last seen, she obviously placed a change of clothes into that backpack that was found. Ok...it starting to make a little sense. Did the analysts find any finger prints from her car?"

Jack shook his head sitting down across from Roy. "No all they got were partials unfortunately."

"Damnit!" Roy voiced loudly hitting her desk in aggravation.

"Well...if it makes you feel any better, these items were found not far from where she was last seen."

"It probably was Vincent. Whoever he is." Roy stated.

"But follow me I have to show you some more CCTV." Jack said as Roy followed close behind. He cued up the footage just before Morgan entered the elevator. They saw Morgan pressing the buttons frantically again looking behind her and as the doors opened, there was a hand that shot out yanking her in. Jack rewound and paused the video just as the hand came into view.

"You see that?"

Roy leaned in and could clearly see a hand that practically yanked Morgan inside.

"Oh my gosh...so now we know...she was abducted," Roy said allowed covering her mouth in shock. "But that doesn't explain why she's not seen again on tape." Roy added.

"But look this will. Look at this guy." Jack pointed to a man carrying a duffle bag out of the elevators and heading outside. They saw the man walk to a vehicle that Roy recognized from earlier popping open the trunk the duffle bag was on the ground and they could faintly notice it move and wiggle around slightly. The man shoved the bag into the trunk and all the while they were hopeful that the man would look up before the car sped away. But the baseball cap he wore made it that much more difficult. As the car was speeding away miraculously, the license plate came into focus for just a split second.

"Oh wow that's great, let's run the plates and see who owns this car." Roy suggested on the edge of her seat as Jack put the plate into the database. The computer was doing a search which felt like an eternity to Roy all she wanted was to find Morgan and bring her home. But once the computer displayed who the owner was of that car, Roy's throat felt dry sinking into the pit of her stomach. She began to feel sick and uneasy once she saw that the owner was Carter Lincoln BeauCannon.

'We might be dead by tomorrow'

Soko

Ginger lie awake in bed watching the ceiling. She placed her hand on her stomach thinking of the life she was creating inside of her. The life that she would give to another human being and that thought made Ginger happy and calm, but at the same time scared and tense. She looked over at Drew who was sleeping seeming like he didn't have anything to worry about, not a care or worry in the world. Ginger sighed a single tear streaming on the side of her freckled cheek remembering the messages she read. All she wanted was for him to give her all of his love. Looking at him knowing that he was the love of her life she didn't want to judge him because she wanted to believe he had a good heart. But she couldn't help thinking if he wasn't ready for love the same as she was then how could he possibly be ready for anything? Be ready for life? Ginger looked at the ceiling once more playing and counting through all of the memories, all of the sorrow, and all of the pain that was adding scars to her heart. When she looked at him all that could ring allowed in her ears was that he wasn't ready now. She placed her hand on her stomach once more and closed her eyes creating more tears and a steady river down her ears and her neck. Ginger didn't believe that he understood as well as her that she wanted his love now and wasn't willing to wait any longer because for all they knew they could be dead by tomorrow.

She knew that eventually he was going to find out about the life she was carrying if she did or didn't tell him. Ginger wondered what was he so scared of? They've been together for a while and she didn't want to believe she was wasting her time with the wrong person. But then again, maybe that was her fate.

Chapter Twenty-four

Roy was kneeling on the front stoop of her condominium tying her pink running shoes tightly around her foot. She stood up and began to do some stretching for a warm up before she took her three-mile jog. Roy took out her I pod clipping it to the side of her yoga pants and began to jog placing the ear buds in place. She jogged on the leaf covered sidewalk path and out from behind the big oak trees onto the main pavement. Roy gave a friendly wave to her neighbors who were passing her by. Roy smiled as she could feel the fresh warm air fill her lungs. She was wondering since it was such a nice day if she should take her normal route or take a different one. But then she remembered the episode on 48-hour mystery she was watching last night and just stuck with her normal route. Roy never understood cop shows. None of them that she had seen never were realistic. It baffled her mind that if cops were really that smart as they are on t.v. then there would have been a lot more cases solved. Roy suddenly feels her phone begin to vibrate in her pocket and she answers jogging at a slower pace.

"Hello?"

"Oh well hi." A deep soft voice came from over the speaker that she didn't recognize which caused her to stop jogging.

"Who is this?"

"Who do you think?"

"I don't know that's why I'm asking…look if this is some prank call bullshi-."

"It's me…the man who was just so kind enough to write you those checks…by the way did you cash them?" Roy began to look around frantically observing her surroundings wondering if she was being followed.

"How the hell did you get this number? You know what, it doesn't even matter. I'm onto you Carter, we know you're involved with

Morgan Stasney's disappearance."

She heard the man laugh which got her more pissed off.

"Is that so? Well that doesn't ring a bell sorry to say."

"We have your vehicle on tape with Morgan in it you bastard. We know you're guilty."

"Oh really?" Carter chuckled and Roy rolled her eyes.

"Yes, and you will be brought to justice and prosecuted, I promise you." Roy threatened her voice strong and firm. "And since we both know the truth, tell me where she is and we can end this right here right now."

"I'm sorry it's just I'm afraid I don't have any answers for you." Carter stated calmly sighing so relaxed.

"Her family wants to bring her home. They've already been hurt enough." Roy raised her voice upset with his demeanor.

"You really are a piece of work...Anna...if you're so convinced that I had something to do with it...then prove it." He hung up before Roy could say anything more. She pulled the phone away from her staring at it, horrified. She questioned, how in the world he knew her first name. The only person that's ever called her Anna was her mother. Roy squeezed the phone in her hand feeling a resentment spark burning inside her core. She really wanted to know who this guy was and what he wanted from her. And even worse, if he could get all of this information about her so easily, what else was he capable of doing. Regardless, Roy wanted this goose chase to stop, but something was cautioning her that it wouldn't be that easy.

'Hanging On
(White sea remix)'

Active child

Nibbling on her pencil Sophie was trying hard to remember the correct formula for a math problem. Math was her weakest subject and she absolutely hated it. It was difficult for her to concentrate because all she could think about was what occurred the other night. Sophie still couldn't believe it actually happened. It felt so real, so right, and so good. She looked around the room at the other students, and almost everyone looked either confused or so prepared and ready they were just scribbling away at their paper. She glanced up at the clock and saw that it was nearly 10 minutes before the period would end.

Shit. Sophie said in her head. She looked down at her test and saw that she only had one page done out of three. She hurried up and tried to figure out the math problem without the formula and guessed her answer hoping it was correct. She hurriedly turned the page and saw that it was a word problem and she let out a sigh of frustration. When it came to word problems Sophie could give less of a damn.

Who gives a fuck how many plates Susie needs to bring to the party if everyone brings two each. Why can't she just call everyone and tell them that she'll just bring the damn plates? You know what I'm just gonna write: 'who cares I'm not going to the party that's susie's problem.' Sophie guessed on all of the other problems and hoped for the best.

"Ok class pencils down pass up your tests." The teacher said standing up beginning to collect the papers row by row. The bell rang as Sophie passed hers to the front and she grabbed her bag quickly making her way to the bus. She didn't want to run into Marribell because she didn't feel like dealing with her at all today; and she had a major headache. But it was to no avail some way some how the heavens made sure that she would run into Marribell before she left.

"Hey Soph!" Marribell yelled weaving her way through crowds of students and teachers. Sophie heard her perfectly clear but she kept walking hoping that if she got on the bus she would be safe and away from her. But Marribell caught up with her anyhow grabbing Sophie's shoulder wheeling her around.

"Hey Soph didn't you hear me calling you silly goose?"

"Nope." Sophie said monotone looking uninterested.

"You wanna come over with me to Charlie's house?" Marribell squealed.

"Umm...no thanks I gotta catch the bus so-."

"Oh no that's fine I can drive you. My mom let me borrow the car this week so you can just ride with me jelly bean!" Marribell grabbed Sophie's hand pulling her along like a wagon. Marribell plopped in the driver side taking her rainbow colored car keys out. Sophie just shook her head putting her seat belt on wondering what kind of fashion statement Marribell was trying to make with bright yellow rain boots, tomato red pants, and a stripped t shirt.

"So Soph! How was your day?"

"Fine."

"Oh mine was great! In art class we were making these sculptures but for some reason mine didn't look like all of the others...isn't that weird?"

"Yup...sure is." Sophie said plainly.

For the rest of the ride it just consisted of Marribell humming the tune of summer breeze by the seals and crofts and Sophie wishing that she could just shoot her brains out. Marribell pulled in the drive way cutting the curb making Sophie pop up out of her seat and almost causing the car to tip over.

"Ok we're here let's get movin!" Marribell yelled flopping up the cement steps in her obnoxious boots. She knocked on the door waiting for someone to open it, but no one was there. She knocked on the door again this time pounding yelling,

"HEY! IS ANYONE HOME???!! HELLO???!!" Some dogs in the neighborhood began to bark from her loud fuss. She was about to pound on the door again when Sophie stopped her.

"Can you at least act like you got some sense?" She asked through her teeth trying to be discreet. Marribell laughed and was about to say something until they saw a red mustang convertible pull into the drive way.

"Oh I think that's Charlie!" Marribell stated. Charlie got out of the car. Her short shaggy hair was dyed a deep blue color at the roots and a teal faded color towards the ends.

"Hey guys. Sorry I wasn't here I had to go make an errand real quick." Charlie smiled coming up the stairs giving Marribell a hug.

"Oh no worries," Marribell began, "You remember my cousin Sophie right?" Charlie turned her attention towards her.

"Oh yeah I remember how've you been?" Charlie asked with a smirk pulling Sophie in for a hug.

"Uh…I've been ok…nothing really goin on…" Sophie answered. Charlie smiled with her eyes roaming Sophie up and down which made her a little bit uncomfortable.

"You look beautiful." Charlie commented. All Sophie did was smile as a response and Charlie opened the door.

"Come on in…sorry about the mess I forgot you were comin over." Charlie's voice faintly flowed from the kitchen. Marribell took a seat on the sofa and Sophie sat next to her. She looked around and saw a bunch of antiques and paintings covering the majority of the room's circumference. Sophie was puzzled about the fact that there wasn't a single photo anywhere in sight of Charlie, Entino, or their parents. She found that a little strange and the dinginess of the house to be unsettling. However, she did enjoy the smell of after rain and dew streaming through the open curtained windows. Sophie then observed the furniture which matched the atmosphere of the house, dull and faint.

"So you guys wanna watch a movie or something?" Charlie asked sitting in the love seat adjacent to them.

"Sure! Do you wanna watch one Soph?"

Sophie just shrugged.

"I don't care we can do whatever." She responded leaning back on the sofa wishing she was at home taking a nap.

"Well we can just see what's on t.v." Charlie suggested turning it on with the remote. Sophie sat up when she heard the back screen door open and slam shut. Entino walked into the room carrying a brown bag, wearing black jeans and a white over shirt exposing his toned bare body. Sophie tried not to make it obvious she was staring.

"Where've you been?" Charlie demanded. Entino took one last drag of his cigarette before disposing of it.

"Out." He simply said going upstairs, Sophie's eyes followed him her body feeling a tingling sensation. Her mind bringing her back to the exotic heated moment they shared in the bathroom. She clutched onto the tan leather sofa wishing that she was clutching onto him and it was difficult to ignore.

"Where's the bathroom?" Sophie leaned over asking Charlie.

"Oh well there's one down here but for some reason it doesn't flush, but there's one upstairs at the end of the hall." At first, Sophie didn't get up trying her best to get back the strength in her legs; but somehow she managed. She slowly made her way up the creaking staircase eyeing the bathroom once she reached the hall. Sophie didn't see Entino anywhere and because of that; she was scared to move but she didn't know why not seeing him would stop her. Sophie suddenly heard music coming from the room next to the bathroom and made her way down following the sound of the music without even thinking. She stood in the doorway and saw Entino laying in bed listening to music with his head phones and his eyes closed. He opened them and turned the music down once he noticed her. And they both just stared at each other, neither one creating a word, a sound, or a whisper.

Sophie walked over to a desk sitting in front of the window taking a seat in the chair. The awkwardness kept growing and growing until Entino stood up walking over to Sophie till he was standing directly in front of her. She looked up at him, her eyes innocent and glassy from the glare. He ran his hand through her long hair and gentle locks and

Sophie closed her eyes. She laid her hands on his pants and exhaled a gasp when he lifted her up in his arms ramming her against the wall. At times, he was tempestuous with her, but Sophie liked it. He continued to rub and caress the side of her face. Sophie closed her eyes once more placing one hand on his following the movements threading through her hair. Entino tilted in and began to whisper delicately in her ear.

"Touch me." His lips brushing against her ear and down to her neck. Sophie felt his abs, her fingers going over each crevice, each muscle, consecutively. Her hands moved onto his broad shoulders gripping his thin shirt, tightly. Entino guided her legs into his grasp firmly forcing her up on the wall even more. He leaned in placing a tender kiss on her quivering lips. His strong hands traveled along her body gripping her hips so securely, Sophie felt like her breaths were scarce, weightily being pressed out of her lungs. With each kiss they shared, Sophie could feel her stomach churning into knots. Their kisses became more eager by the minute, their embrace performing the same. He stopped and their bodies touched; their breath interlocking. Sophie was keened on his valiant yellow eyes and he stared back just the same stroking her soft cheek. His touch was intoxicating and Sophie could never get enough. She leaned forward giving him a soft kiss and it sent an immense chill down her spine.

She studied his face in every detail wondering why he was attracted to her so much, why he wanted her so much. She loved the way he made her feel. He had such an effect on her even if they weren't touching.

"I see you came back for round two." He said in a hushed tone. Sophie rolled her eyes smiling.

"And?"

"I like that."

Sophie blushed breaking eye contact.

"I like a woman that goes after what she wants." Entino looked at her deep into her eyes almost reaching her soul it felt like. Easing her down, he led her over to the bed and they laid side by side stuck in a spell by each other's gaze. Sophie felt that time was standing still when she was with Entino, like she had an eternity to be around him and nothing else in the world mattered.

"What else do you like?" Sophie was intrigued getting more comfortable with his stare.

"A woman who knows how to please...how to take control." Entino stated.

"So...if she's bossy...you like that?"

He smirked and snickered. "Only in moments of intimacy, remember when you told me not to stop the last time you let me have my way with you?"

"So, you like that?"

"Like having my way with you...or a woman taking control?"

"Well...I guess both..." Her voice straggled off, and she hoped this warm delicate moment wouldn't be ruined by her awkwardness.

His eyes trailed her body from head to toe. And every time his gazed transitioned to another area, her body became feeble.

"Yes." He answered her simply watching her eyes much deeper than he had before.

Sophie's mouth was gaped open speechless. "Wow...you're so... straightforward..."

"So I've been told."

Sophie's eyes darted away from his feeling vulnerable to him. Did she like it? Did she hate it? Maybe even love that feeling? She was torn and feeling that way bothered her. For whatever reason, she suddenly got the urge to become bold, just like him. Ask him what was on his mind, basic and simple. She knew that it may make her look stupid, but she didn't care. The torn feeling consuming her every thought eating away at her.

"What is it you want from me?" Sophie shot suddenly and she bit and pursed her lips. It felt like her body was more than ready and her mind couldn't keep up. She didn't intend to get her answers using that question. Sophie could tell Entino was attempting to find out why she would ask such a random question. But when she looked into his yellow eyes, it was clear that he respected her assertiveness and for cutting right to the chase. He smiled.

"I don't want anything from you." He answered plainly. Sophie knew he was testing her. Seeing if she had enough nerve to keep pressing towards her intention.

She wasn't certain if she had enough courage to ask more of him. But when she looked at him, she saw he wanted her to. The way he kept glaring at her keeping a calm face not looking the least bit intimated.

"Why did you do what you did at the party then?" She could feel her heart skipping beats her forehead starting to become warm.

"Why did you let me?" He inquired ever so daring.

Not anticipating such a question, caused Sophie to be thrown off guard.

"I…" She began and she saw him smirk. "I didn't…I…you made me by locking me in there."

"Oh, you're so right…I made you moan my name, made you so satisfied you begged me for more. I made you say all of those things?"

"No…I…that's not what I meant…"

"One thing is for sure though…if your cousin hadn't interrupted, you would've kept going…" She looked up at him and was immediately pierced with his mysterious eyes and she froze.

"You don't know that." She exclaimed.

"Don't pretend you didn't enjoy it." He insisted tugging her toward him, their faces inches from one another.

"Why do you love making me feel the way you do?" She shyly met his gaze, he placed her in a trance state.

"Because I like you." He leaned in giving her a deep kiss touching the side of her face. She pulled herself to him more clinging onto his shirt not wanting to stop this moment of affection. She could feel her lip start to bleed a little as it kept brushing against his spiked snake bite piercing. But for some reason, she loved that and didn't care, even if his kisses were painful.

'Acres of fire'

House of Wolves

It takes nine months to create a human being inside a woman's womb. And for most of them, those nine months are of pure and utter bliss. But for Ginger Spring however, she was not one of them. Her stomach is now, before she knew it, protruding away from the rest of her body and the sight disgusted her. She always dreamt of having children with Drew one day, but not under these circumstances and she hated herself for it. Ginger turned to see her swollen stomach from a side view and there was no hiding it anymore anyone could tell by looking at her that she was pregnant. It was times like these Ginger wished she was a bigger girl so that if she did get pregnant it would just look like she gained a lot of weight. She ran her frail hands across her mound wondering how in the world she was going to go to school like this. Her mother opened the door slowly peeking in.

"Hi honey how are you?" Her mother came by her side giving her hug. Ginger was relieved that at least her mother was supportive if no one else was going to be. She was very grateful for that because she knew that only a lucky few get this kind of support from their parents. Ginger held onto her mother tightly letting her tears fall and soak the shoulder of her blouse.

"It's going to be ok sweetie." Her mother reassured her softly stroking her strawberry blonde hair.

"No it's not mom…they're all gonna laugh at me…I mean look…" Ginger pulled away pointing at her reflection in the mirror. Her mom grabbed both of Ginger's hands turning Ginger's attention on her.

"Look…honey I know this is tough…I know…but it is what it is and we're just gonna have to deal with it. Now I'll drive you to school ok? Just focus on what you need to do."

Ginger looked at her, still not positive about anything. She knew that staying home wasn't an option because she's already missed so many days.

"Trust me…it's gonna be ok…now get dressed and I'll be waiting for you in the car." Her mother left the room and Ginger looked at herself in the mirror once again. She knew it was wrong but she wanted the baby inside of her to die before birth. The thought moved Ginger in such a way that she didn't even recognize herself anymore. She never, in all of her life wished anyone were dead. She shook the thought out of her mind grabbing her backpack to meet her mother in the driveway. The whole ride there Ginger's body became weaker and weaker; her mind became stiller and stiller. She tried not to think about where she was going. Instead, she imagined herself just driving to the park with her mother like she always did when she was little. But her imagination soon came to an end once she saw the school appear in the window. Never, in her whole life, has Ginger ever been this scared to go to school. She didn't move she just sat there staring out the window at all of the cliques making their way in the building.

"Honey." Her mother said laying a hand on Ginger's shoulder startling her out of her thoughts.

"It's ok…I'll be here to pick you up after." Ginger looked at her mother one last time before giving her hug and reluctantly getting out of the car. The one thing that made her calm somewhat was her hand behind her still touching the car handle. She felt lost once her safe place vanished from her grasp and from that point on Ginger knew it was just her now. Immediately students, even teachers, began to stare and for a moment, Ginger's first instinct was to run and just be swept away. But something stopped her and she walked to the entrance; her eyes not making contact with anyone but the cement. The sidewalk was the only one she felt wasn't passing judgment. She could hear people faintly whispering and she knew all eyes were on her; people were saying, 'Oh my gosh are you serious?', 'Wow what a slut,' 'Tramp', 'fucking whore', 'she's a dirty skank.'

Ginger had tears in the back of her throat making her feel like a joke, the laughing stalk of the whole school. The closer she got to the door, the more horrible things she heard ringing in her head. She made it to her first class not looking at anyone the whole time. And she eased herself in the desk barely fitting because of her big belly. Not only was sitting in the desk unnerving but people staring, laughing, and whispering when they walked in wasn't helping at all. And after class the teacher wanted to speak with her.

"Have a seat Ginger." Ms. Abola said gesturing to a chair beside her desk. Ginger did so, still not making eye contact. The tile on the floor was her friend.

"Ginger," Ms. Abola began leaning forward laying a hand on Ginger's shaky pale thigh. And for the first time today, she actually looked someone in the eye.

"Don't worry about making up any of the work you missed ok? I'll take care of it."

"But...but what about the final??? What am I gona-."

"Don't worry about it ok? You just focus on you right now. If it makes you feel any better...I was a pregnant teen too. So I know exactly what you're feeling right now."

Ginger's eyes widening with shock.

"What??? I would never expect that."

Ms. Abola laughed putting her short black curls behind her ears. "Ha, I know right? But somehow I made it. And if you ever need anything...or if you think you can't find a friend, you know where to find me ok?"

Ginger wiped away a few single tears.

"Thank you Ms. Abola." She stood up giving her an embrace.

"You're welcome hun." She said tapping her back which made Ginger feel hopeful about her situation.

"See you tomorrow." Ginger said smiling for the first time that day. But that quickly disappeared once she submerged herself in the hall of critics. She felt like she was on display at an art gallery, people just pointing, laughing, and staring at her. She quickly began to walk away not knowing where she was going just walking to get away.

Ginger bumped into Cecil and Issac who still looked just as creepy and just as pale as usual. They both looked her up and down shaking their bony pale faces.

"Tisk, tisk tisk." Cecil stated still shaking her head with disappointment.

"I know...it's a shame...she just couldn't keep her legs closed till marriage." Issac remarked. Cecil began to walk towards her laying her ghostly hand on Ginger's shoulder.

"You couldn't at least wait till you got out of high school," Cecil started looking in disbelief and shame. "May god have mercy on your soul." They both walked away leaving Ginger stranded in her own circle detached from everyone else's. Even Ginger's so called friends walked right past her with the same uniform look on their faces.

Ginger's eyes began to swell with tears and she began to walk quickly through the hall passing everyone hearing laughs, gasps, and faint whispers. She wasn't even looking where she was going just as long as she got out of sight. She turned the corner to walk out of a side door when she ran into Slyder.

"Whoa hey, what's wrong Ginger?" He asked stopping her momentum. She turned to look at him and his expression turned into concern once he saw her wet puffy face.

"Whoa hey what happened?" Ginger kept sniffling trying to speak but it hurt to force the words out.

"I...just...wanna...get...out of here." Ginger cried between sniffles. Slyder wrapped his arm around her.

"Ok let's go." He walked her out onto the lawn until they reached the student parking lot. And Ginger calmed down a little bit once they were both sitting in his car. But Ginger was still crying and sniffling. Slyder grabbed a tissue box from in the back handing it to her and she quickly blew her nose.

"Just take your time its ok." He comforted her gently stroking her arm.

"I'm just...so...scared Slyder...I don't know what I'm gonna do." Ginger wined laying her head in her unstable hands. Slyder lifted her chin up to make eye contact.

"Don't worry Ginger...I'm here...I'll take care of you." Slyder grabbed her hand feeling so promising and genuine to Ginger, and that is something she's had always desired from Drew but had never gotten.

'Here Before'

Lissie

Awakening from the sun beaming through the white curtains, Ginger's eyes slowly opened, hazel and reflecting against the light. She sat up on her elbows and saw Slyder drawing something on a working table. He turned around when he heard Ginger begin to move from under the sheets. He smiled joining her at her side.

"Good morning." Slyder smiled at her; the flushed yellow light glaring one side of his body. Ginger smiled back.

"Good morning…I hope me staying the night here wasn't too much of a hassle for you." She said feeling like a bother.

"Oh it's no trouble at all…as long as you're ok." He sat next to her and Ginger felt safe. She glanced down at her ankles which were swollen red tumors latching onto her feet. She let out a gasp.

"What is it?" Slyder asked reaching out his hand in case she needed support.

"My ankles…" He looked down at them.

"Here." He placed Ginger's arm hanging around his neck and he lifted her legs from underneath sliding her into the soft sheets. "You just have to keep your feet elevated and you should be alright." Slyder assured her gathering pillows stacking them under Ginger's horribly puffed-up feet. He covered her with the soft blankets and Ginger nestled herself comfortably. Slyder smiled at her walking back to his drawing.

"So what are you drawing over there?" Ginger wondered.

"Oh…just a sketch…I'm not quite sure exactly what it's gonna be yet." He turned and gave her smile and she did the same. This is what she's yearned for from a guy almost her whole teenage life, just attention, love, and understanding. She looked at Slyder working so diligently and she thought why she couldn't have been with him first. She was going back to memories in her head of the relationship her and Drew shared. Ginger felt foolish. What could she really expect from an immature high school relationship? In a way she couldn't get mad at Drew for acting his age and handling the situation the way he did, but at the same time she didn't understand why taking responsibility for his actions was too much to ask for. She closed her eyes going back to the memory that hurt her the most. She remembered like it was just yesterday, the fighting, the pain, and the hurt.

****

Ginger took a deep breath and opened the door to Drew's bedroom. Trying to think of how she was going to tell him. She saw him on his computer jamming away to his music with his headphones. He didn't hear her walk in and that gave Ginger a little open window of time to run through her response. She half-heartedly approached him and tapped on his shoulder. And she began to count down in her mind the number of seconds she had from the moment she tapped his shoulder to the time he faced her. Drew turned around and smiled at first not noticing her belly. But then his eyes trailed down to her stomach and Ginger wished she had given herself more time.

"What the hell happened to you?" Drew asked repulsively. Ginger's throat was dry and empty like a desert, and she wished that there was more time for her to come up with an answer.

"What do you think happened…I'm pregnant…"

Drew's expression became blank and it looked like he didn't know how to respond.

"Can you say something…?" Ginger asked quietly.

"What am I supposed to say?" He asked raising his voice standing up and towering over her. She backed up feeling intimated and scared.

"How about something like I'm excited we're going to have a baby I don't know…just something." Ginger began to raise her voice as well. Drew blinked with total shock a couple times and seemed at a loss.

"But I'm not. Why the hell didn't you tell me when you found out?!" Drew yelled backing her up against the dresser and Ginger turned away from him afraid. She had never seen this side of Drew before.

"I was scared ok?! I was scared! I didn't know what to do, it's not like I planned this!" She began to gather up the courage to stand up for herself.

"Well no the hell duh Ginger…god…why couldn't you just go to the clinic?"

"Well you said that if I was pregnant we'd take care of it…"

"I didn't mean that we would take care of it as in raise the baby…I meant abort it."

Ginger shuttered at that word. She may not have wanted the baby, but she would never think about killing it. She began to shake her head with disappointment in her eyes.

"Abort it." Drew commanded.

"I can't…how could you say that with such carelessness. This could be your son…or even your daughter…and you wanna kill it?… You're sick." Ginger told him heading to the door to leave but Drew gripped onto her arm yanking her back to face him.

"What's the point in keeping it…if I don't want it?" Drew asked; his eyes dark and lifeless like the bottom of the ocean.

"Don't touch me… I've been here before with you and I can't take this anymore ok?" Ginger jerked her arm out of his tight grasp

"Just get out…and take that thing with you." Drew said moving her out into the hall slamming the door shut in Ginger's face. She pinched her eyes closed and waterfall of tears tumbled down her face. She left and wasn't intending on having anything to do with Drew any longer.

****

Just thinking of that very day made Ginger feel as horrible as she did then. But she knew where she was right now was her refuge, away from harm, away from judgment, and away from him. Ginger put her hand on her stomach running it up and down over the stretch marked skin. She was happy to have Drew out of her life. Nevertheless, she couldn't help but think that maybe he was right, she should have aborted it. But Ginger believed everything happens for a reason she just had to trust that she will know which way to go and be able to shine again.

'Nice weather for ducks'

Lemon Jelly

Marribell's weirdness seemed to grow more and more each day. Sophie was sitting in Marribell's room bored out of her mind looking at her trying on all of these obnoxious combinations of clothing.

"So what do you think about this Soph?!" She asked twirling around in a yellow dress that looked too tight for her, rainbow leggings, and cowboy boots. Sophie blinked 10 times in a row in confusion and horror.

"Um…which part? The top the middle or the bottom…because all of it is fucking hideous." Sophie said in monotone slouching back in Marribell's unicorn pillows folding her arms.

"Oh stop it…I think it looks nice. I might wear this for my birthday party."

"Yeah you should all you need now is bright red pigtails and a basket full of goodies!" Sophie said sarcastically using fake enthusiasm.

"Hmm…I don't think it would go well with this outfit do you?" She asked posing in the mirror.

"Yeah sure why not? You got everything else on."

"No I don't I have more clothes in the closet. I'm gonna go and try some more on."

"No!" Sophie said barely cutting Marribell off.

"Why not?"

"Because I'm sick of this joke of a fashion show and I'm going home." Sophie said climbing out of bed about to leave.

"But wait! Don't you wanna go outside or something?" Marribell offered excitedly.

"What…why the hell would I wanna go outside it's raining."

Marribell turned around peering out of her 'My Little Pony' curtains. "Yeah but so…we can pretend to be ducks or something jumping in the puddles!" She squealed but Sophie didn't look impressed.

"Ok well you can go outside and look like a fool acting like a duck, but I'm going home because I don't give a fuck." She began to leave but Marribell zoomed in front of her grabbing her arm flailing Sophie down the stair case.

They both dashed through the drizzling drops of rain hopping in the car.

"Where the hell are you taking me?" Sophie demanded an answer watching Marribell start up the engine and driving off.

"I don't know…hm…maybe we can go…to…oh! That amusement park is in town we should go there!" She picked up her speed and Sophie was surprised that she didn't get a ticket for the whole ride. But then again, she couldn't blame the cops. If she saw Marribell's outfit through the window she wouldn't pull her over either. She heard the brakes squeal to a halt in front of the amusement park.

"It's been so long since I've been to one." Marribell said admiring all of the fun rides. Sophie just rolled her eyes getting out of the car; Marribell ran up towards the ticket booth to join the line of customers. Sophie took her time walking over to join her wishing she could just drop dead.

"Aren't you excited??!!" Maribell screeched with joy causing a few customers in line to turn around with a jumbled look.

"Oh my gosh yeah! This is just how I wanna to spend my time. In the rain, with you, at an amusement park! Whoopee!" Sophie sarcastically said matching Marribell's level of joy. Once they approached the ticket booth Marribell glanced down at the prices.

"Ticket for two please!" She asked. The older woman with poufy white hair behind the desk look displeased with Marribell just as much as Sophie did.

"That'll be $12." She answered with her scraggly scratchy drone voice. Marribell swung her Joe bag banging it obnoxiously on the counter digging around for cash.

"Ok hold on…I just gotta get…some money." She said pulling out crumpled dollars one at a time. "Ok well that's one…two…three… four…" She began to count pulling out more crumbled up dollar bills. If Sophie didn't know any better she'd think she did stripping as a side job.

"Ok here's another one…so that's five." She said pennies and quarters dropping everywhere still digging around in her bag.

"Oh here's a five dollar bill. Ha! What'd ya know? I didn't even know I had that in here." She said giving a big grin to the lady behind the counter, but the lady still looked unimpressed. After a few more minutes of Marribell digging around for cash she finally had enough money handing it over to the lady.

"Here's two tickets… have fun." The lady said with no enthusiasm. Marribell snatched Sophie's hand entering the loud park and she looked around and observed a bunch of screaming kids whining about not being able to get on the marry-go-round. And she was also crying inside along with them for help to get away from her cousin.

"You wanna go on the tilt-a-whirl???" Marribell said still dragging Sophie along walking towards it.

"I really don't care." She replied feeling like her hand was losing circulation.

"Ok let's go get on it!" Marribell started to change her pace to a light jog causing Sophie to feel like a rag doll. She finally was capable to get out of Marribell's tight grasp once they were in line waiting. When it was their turn to get on the ride, Marribell didn't even wait to give the other riders time to get off; she just pushed passed all of them forcing them all to split like the red sea. Sophie put her head in her hand following her thinking that they all probably thought she was loony tunes and escaped from the nut house. And the outfit wasn't helping.

Marribell secured herself tight into the open slot and Sophie reluctantly did the same. They waited for all of the other's to secure themselves and have the operator check to make sure everyone was held in place safely. When the man reached Marribell he stopped and began to rearrange the buckle making it tighter.

"GEEZE MAGEEZE WHAT ARE YOU TRYING TO DO?? SPLIT ME IN HALF????!!" Marribell spazzed out at full volume and all Sophie could do was look away and pretend she didn't know her.

"Um...no..." The guy simply said getting off the ride leaving everyone glaring at Marribell, the colorful one of the bunch. The ride began to twist slowly at first until it began spinning faster and quicker. Sophie really didn't like this ride she always had a headache afterwards and she didn't know why she even agreed to get on it. But she was sure Marribell felt the complete opposite since she was just screaming and laughing having a good time. Once the ride was over Sophie was the first one to get off and Marribell once again forced people out of her way joining Sophie at her side.

"WOW! Wasn't that great?!" She screeched piercing Sophie's ears.

"Why are you yelling?" She asked simply observing all of the attention she placed on them.

"I'm not yelling. This is how I talk."

"Well try to speak softer....preash." Sophie said walking over to the concession stand and seating area.

"Oh great idea Soph! We should probably grab something to eat!" Marribell said rushing off to get food and Sophie just shook her head sitting there wishing this whole excursion could just be over and done with.

What did I do to deserve this kind of embarrassment? I hope we're leaving after this because I'm done dealing with her shit. And look here she comes trying to balance all of this food in her hand. God only knows why she didn't grab a tray. I guess that'd just be too easy. Marribell reached the table dumping all of the food she had purchased.

"Ok so here's your stuff." She said handing her a slice of cheese pizza, a bottled drink, and a donut that looked hard as a rock.

"And this is my stuff." She said plopping a seat on the bench devouring her food like it was going to grow legs and run off. Sophie glanced around in humiliation. Even the kids who were screaming stopped and gave a look.

"Yum yum yum." Marribell said with food stuffed in her cheek and pieces hanging out of her mouth. Sophie just stared horrified. She looked like a wild beast. Sophie leaned in reaching her hand out to touch Marribell's arm.

"Ummm…Marribell." Sophie spoke softly. "I think you've already humiliated me enough with that outfit you're wearing from the Salvation Army. And I really don't need you to sit here and CHOMP ON YOUR FOOD LIKE A FUCKING IDIOT CAUSING ALL OF THIS ATTENTION ON US!" Sophie yelled drawing more onlookers.

She stopped chewing looking confused at Sophie.

"What's wrong with you?"

"What??….HAHAHA! WHATS WRONG WITH ME? YOU OF ALL PEOPLE ARE GONNA ASK WHAT'S WRONG WITH ME?? WHO LOOKS LIKE THE NORMAL ONE HERE? THE ONE WEARING APPROPRIATE CLOTHES OR THE ONE WITH THE FUCKING CLOWN SUIT???" Parents looked appalled and covered their children's ears gathering up their belongings and leaving.

"Sophie please shh…just sit down." Marribell calmly said now eating her food with a little bit more decency. Sophie calmed down taking a seat on the bench. She put her head in her hands once more imagining she was somewhere else.

"Oh hey did you hear about that park the town was gonna reconstruct?" Marribell asked randomly.

Sophie shook her head no. "Why?"

"Well because I remember when I was babysitting one day most of the equipment was broken. So I'm kind of excited about being able to bring the kids over to it once it's done." Marribell said eating a spoon full of ice cream. Sophie just shrugged.

"Oh my goodness Marribell…you look more beautiful than I remember."

They both heard a voice say and Sophie turned around to see. Her mouth gaped open.

Please don't tell me this is another one of her drop dead gorgeous ex-boyfriends.

"Awh stop it Devon." Marribell blushed when he took a seat next to her.

"Well Devon this is my cousin Sophie, and Sophie this is my ex-hold on

boyfriend Devon." Sophie just smirked and he smiled at her.

"I can't even begin to tell you how much I miss you." Devon said sweetly and Marribell giggled.

"Oh please. It wasn't going to work. And plus I just wanted to test out my other options."

OPTIONS?! This girl had fucking options?? Looking like that? There's no way. Why are all of these hot model type guys attracted to her??? With her looking like that she better take what she can get. Pssh...options... unbelievable.

"Well I gotta get goin...you have my number so call me sometime." He said winking at her walking away. Marribell turned around shaking her head looking flattered and smiling. Sophie stood up and began to walk away and Marribell shouted after her.

"Wait! Where are you goin silly crocodile?"

"To jump off a cliff." Sophie said plainly.

"Oh...ok...I don't know why you'd wanna do that but I'll come with you!" She yelled following after her.

Chapter Thirty-One

The fact that you can't please everybody is a part of this world just as much as nature itself. And at first, Ginger refused to accept and understand that fact. But the closer and closer she got to motherhood, she felt that in a way it helped her. It helped her to understand people and situations well, and to forgive and forget people that have hurt you. Even though she may be able to count the positive things on one hand, as opposed to negative things, that didn't bother Ginger anymore. From this point on she had made a promise to herself that no matter how hard life got, she wasn't going to let it break her. She ran the soothing bath water over her legs soaking her sensitive, frail body to try and relax. Slyder peeked in the candle lit bathroom and Ginger smiled at him.

"I brought some more towels in case you needed them." He said laying them next to the tub.

"Thank you." Ginger said feeling extremely weighed down and exhausted.

"You ok? Need anything else?" Slyder offered.

"Yeah…could you stay in here with me a while? I just wanted some company." She pleaded while running the water over her stomach. He smiled and closed the door sitting on the edge of the tub. She smiled at him glad that he decided to stay. But she couldn't help but wonder why he was being so nice to her. Who was she to him but just a girl he knew from school. Did he feel bad for her because she was pregnant? Or did he feel obligated because he considers her a friend? Ever since he's been taking care of her she's always wondered that. She gasped softly when Slyder unexpectedly began to scrub and wash her feet and ankles.

"Why are you doing this?" Ginger asked, not even thinking before she spoke. Slyder looked at her confused.

"Doing what?"

"Taking care of me. It's not that I don't appreciate it or anything…I just…wonder." Slyder smiled, golden strands falling in front of his eyes, and he continued to wash her.

"Well why not? I mean it doesn't take a lot to be nice to someone… right?" Slyder looked over at her waiting for an answer and Ginger looked down at the suds and bubbles gathering around her belly.

"Yeah…you're right…it's just…I guess I never expected any kind of help…from anyone."

"Well I said I'd take care of you didn't I?" He winked charmingly smiling at her and she began to play with her hair thinking of what to say.

"Thank you…I promise…once I have the baby and everything you don't have to worry about doing anything for me."

"No…I want you to stay…I mean you can stay if you want to but if you wanna go home that's fine too." He smiled once more lifting her leg up in his strong hands beginning to wash her some more. She watched the water trickle down and it reminded her of her own tears she shed.

"Thank you." Ginger was very grateful for him.

It saddened her that Drew couldn't be in Slyder's place right now, taking care of her and paying her his undivided attention to make sure she had everything she needed.

"So what are you gonna name it if it's a girl?" He asked washing her other leg.

"Hmmm….you know…I've never thought about it. Maybe I'll name her something like…Alice…or…Salina…something like that." Slyder nodded in agreement.

"Yeah those are lovely names. What about if it's a boy?"

"Hmmm…that's hard because I really want a girl that way I can dress her up like a doll." Ginger smiled excitedly thinking about it.

"Heh and what's wrong with boys? You can't dress up a boy?" Slyder asked teasingly and Ginger laughed.

"No that's not what I meant. You can but not in a dress." Ginger clarified and Slyder smiled placing her leg down in the warm water softly.

"Are you ready to get up?" He asked her standing and gathering a towel. Ginger nodded grabbing on to the handle bars for support pulling her heavy body out of the water. She reached for the towel and Slyder wrapped her in a cocoon of warmth. He placed Ginger's arm around his neck and he grabbed her wet pruned hand helping her step out of the bath. She smiled and went to the guest bedroom where she witnessed that there was a night gown that Slyder laid out on the bed for her.

He never forgot one single detail and always made for certain that she was at her highest level of comfort and thinking about that made her smile. She dried herself off and began to lather her body in lotion. She then took the soft night gown placing it over her head letting it fall over her body. Even though being a pregnant teen was sometimes viewed as shameful, Ginger was proud of herself for doing all she could do for her child. And she wished that Drew felt the same. She caught herself from time to time considering bringing him back into her life and try to work it out. But at least she still had her baby shower to look forward to, and she couldn't wait to finally celebrate and be happy.

Chapter Thirty-Two

Ginger was sending out invitations for her baby shower in the mail. She was running through the list of guests in her head double checking to see if she didn't miss anyone. But then she remembered she hasn't spoken to Sophie ever since she transferred so she decided to give her a call excited to hear her best friend's voice again.

"Hello?" Sophie answered.

"Hi Soph it's me Ginger! How've you been?" She squealed with delight.

"Oh wow Ginger hey! I haven't spoken to you in...like...months how are you?"

"I'm ok...a lot of things going on but I'm alright." She said trying her best not to think about the last couple weeks. Ginger hoped that Sophie wouldn't ask about Drew; she really didn't want to think about that jerk anymore.

"So how are you and Drew doing? Did you guys go to homecoming together or anything?"

Ginger let out a sigh afraid that Sophie would ask anyway.

"Um...well we're not together anymore we broke up a couple weeks ago so..."

"Oh...wow...what happened??" Sophie questioned her. Ginger closed her eyes taking another deep breath struggling to hold back tears; it was still a delicate subject.

"Well...we just...got into an argument and we decided to call it quits. That's all." She lied.

"Oh...that's strange...what was the argument about? Come on give me some details you know I love to hear those." Sophie interrogated further causing Ginger to feel uncomfortable wishing she didn't call in the first place. She was backed into a corner. But she couldn't really get annoyed with Sophie; they did this all the time back when they both attended Vermyear Academy. But Ginger figured what's the harm in telling her the truth? Sophie could be trusted.

"Ok...well...the argument was about..." She took another deep breath building up the courage. "My pregnancy...and I told him that it was his but he didn't want anything to do with me so...he kicked me out." Ginger felt tongue tied and it then became hushed over the phone. All she could hear was background noise amidst them both. But Sophie eventually spoke.

"You're...pregnant??? What are you gonna do now?"

"Well I moved out of my parent's house the day I went over to tell Drew about it thinking he would help me. And I had nowhere else to go. But luckily Slyder let me stay with him for a couple weeks until I have the baby. And then I can go back home." It was silent once more.

"You're staying at Slyder's house??"

"Yeah."

"Why?" Ginger could tell Sophie was beginning to get annoyed with that detail.

"Well he offered and...I accepted."

"Why didn't you just go back to your parent's house?" Sophie cross-examined her and Ginger was beginning to undergo uneasiness again.

"I don't know Sophie, I wasn't really thinking about it. I was just glad to have some place to stay. And he's been helping me out a lot."

"Right...ok...whatever." Sophie said with an irritated tone. Ginger began to speculate whether it was a good idea or not to invite her. But she wanted her best friend to be there with her.

"So...I was wondering if you maybe wanted to come to my baby shower..."

"Where?"

"It's at Slyder's house." She retorted.

"Um...I'll see. When is it?"

"This Saturday."

"Hm...I'll see...I might be busy." Sophie said.

"Ok...well...it starts at 10:00 if you wanna come." Ginger offered.

"Thanks...I'll talk to you later." Sophie said hanging up barely giving Ginger enough time to say goodbye. Sophie was pissed off at her. She really didn't like it all that she was staying over his house. It just made her feel uncomfortable. Sophie was pondering about that almost the whole week until Saturday snuck up on her. But she went anyway and right away regretted it once she was dropped off. She stood there on the lawn with a baby bottle for a gift almost about to change her mind but she went inside anyhow. She saw Ginger's back facing her placing out food dishes on the marble countertop.

Sophie's eyes widened once she took a glimpse of just how immense and wide her stomach had become. She almost didn't recognize her. Ginger saw her and rushed over giving her an embrace.

"I'm so glad you were able to make it." She said happily.

"Here's your gift." Sophie said handing it to her once they parted.

"Thank you. Come on sit down. I was just putting some food out for the other guests."

"Who else is coming?"

"Well mostly my close family and family friends. That's about all."

Sophie nodded looking around at all of the balloons, streamers, and tons of gifts piling over the glass table facing her. More of Ginger's family members walked in greeting her and placing their gifts on the table with the rest. Sophie felt like Ginger was married, living in this house, and having a family with Slyder. The guy Sophie had her first crush with.

"Hey Ginger did you want me to put the cake up here?" Sophie observed Slyder ask like her thoughts had spoken him into existence. He also didn't look the same and Sophie thought maybe it was because he got taller or because she hasn't seen or spoken to him in a while.

"Uh…you can place it right here next to the macaroni salad." She gestured gathering out utensils and napkins like she owned this house. And that's what annoyed Sophie the most; she looked too comfortable for comfort being here with Slyder. And she began to doubt that Ginger had only been staying here for a couple weeks. Sophie crossed her arms laying back into the cushions on the couch looking at everyone smiling, greeting, and laughing with each other. She didn't notice that Slyder had sat next to her until he spoke.

"Hey Sophie…I've missed you." He said softly putting his arm around her. Sophie didn't say anything just stared at the carpet.

"Is something wrong?" Slyder asked pulling her in closer to him until their bodies touched. Sophie just shook her head no still not making eye contact with him.

"Come on don't be like this…why haven't you texted me anymore?" Slyder asked trying his best to make Sophie speak to him.

"I've been busy." Sophie simply stated still not looking at him. He then placed his hand under her chin lifting her head up to face him.

"Busy doing what?"

"Why does it matter?" Sophie spat putting her head back into its original position. Before Slyder could speak Ginger interrupted him.

"Ok everyone thank you so much for coming to my baby shower. Um…please help yourself to food and drinks and then we'll get started with some fun activities!" Ginger announced with a grin.

"Oh Slyder could you help me move these presents over there in the other room?" Ginger asked already moving some of them.

"I'll be back ok?" He said getting up assisting her. Sophie would rather be hanging out with Marribelle than be stuck here feeling like a third wheel. She didn't even know anyone around her besides Ginger and Slyder. The whole event Ginger kept calling on him to help her like he was her husband or something.

I shouldn't have come to this stupid ass party. Should've known once a whore always a whore. Can't teach an old whore new tricks. After all of the pointless games everyone participated in it was time to open gifts. And everyone rushed into the other room to watch and take pictures of her opening them. Sophie got up and joined the crowd and she could care less if she saw her opening them or not.

"Oh my gosh thank you so much Aunt Marie! I love it!" Ginger said under all of the rummaging of wrapping paper and everyone clapped snapping more pictures. She held up an infant pink dress with a plush white bonnet.

"It's so beautiful!" Ginger boasted again. She began unwrapping more presents and everyone gasped and clapped whenever they saw what was under the wrapping paper.

These people are all crazy. They must have been too busy dancing with Mr. Brownstone because I would not be happy and cheery if this was my daughter. I wouldn't even throw her a party I'd be whopping her ass. They act like this is a good thing. It's like oh wow you should be so happy Mrs. Spring your daughter couldn't keep her musty legs closed and got pregnant and she hasn't even gotten her high school diploma. YAY! And they're gonna celebrate about it? All of them are just damn crazy. She later informed Marribelle about all of this after the party sprawled across her Hello Kitty blanket.

"Wow…what????" Marribelle was shocked.

"Yeah I know…she's been a whore all her life so…I guess that's all she knows. I wouldn't be surprised if her mother was one too. Like mother like daughter." Sophie vented.

"Well you didn't talk to Slyder or anything artichoke???" She questioned changing her yoga position on the bright yellow carpet.

"No I only talked to him once. And then after that the whore needed him to "help" her. I'm glad that they helped her get dressed because she probably would have come out naked."

"Well bubble gup, maybe it's better this way."

"Psshh. I don't see how but I guess. I'm just trying to forget about her. She knew that I liked him; she knew that and she did all of this on purpose. Walking around like, 'Oh Slyder come help me with this, oh baby come help me with this, oh my I think the baby's kicking blah blah blah blah. It's like shut the fuck up."

"Well at least she invited you." Marribelle tried to mention a bright side.

"She invited me to rub it in my face. It's probably Slyder's baby for all we know." Sophie sighed in disgust. "Just thinking about it makes me wanna scratch."

"How do you know froggie leg? It might not be."

"Either way she's still a whore. Silly me for thinking she changed."

"Some folks never do. You know what they say different strokes for different folks."

"And different beau's for different hoes." Sophie felt her phone vibrate against her thigh and she was surprised to see that it was a text from Slyder.

Can you meet me?

Where? And for what?

At the knolls because I wanna show you something.

Sophie placed her phone back next to her thigh thinking whether or not she should. What could Slyder possibly have to show her anyway? She sat up off the bed slipping her shoes back on.

"Where you goin lucky ducky?" Marribelle asked now following the movements on a palates CD.

"I'm just gonna run somewhere real quick I'll be right back." Sophie left the room closing the door.

'Jltf'

Moby

S ophie arrived at the knolls taking shelter under a tree from the drizzling rain looking around to see if Slyder was anywhere in sight. She hugged herself shivering wishing by now she had brought a jacket. Sophie noticed his car pull up next to the fence and she walked out from under the tree a little letting him see her. He got out of the car carrying a rolled up white poster board in his hand and hurried over to meet her.

"So what do you want?" She asked through shivers with strings of wet hair hanging in her face.

"I wanted to see you." He told her and Sophie rolled her eyes.

"You got a lot of nerve coming to see me after the stunt you pulled." Slyder looked confused brushing strings of gold back from his view.

"What the hell are you talking about?"

"Oh yeah that's classic let's play the "I don't know game" that's such bullshit!" She yelled.

"No what's bullshit is that I want to see you after all of this time of not talking to you because you kept blowing me off. THAT is bullshit."

"Pssh well excuse me if I had things to do."

"Every day for the past five months?" He questioned.

"You know what just tell me what you want." Sophie sighed.

"Why are you so angry with me? Is this about Ginger staying with me? Is that what it is?" Slyder moved towards her making her back up against the bark her fingers running over the deep rough uneven crevices.

"No...can you just get on with it. What do you want?"

"I was just helping her Sophie. That's it nothing more."

"Yeah ok whatever you say can you just tell me what you want already?"

Slyder sighed and looked down at the board he was carrying.

"I want you to have this." Sophie took the board unrolling it to reveal a picture of Slyder and her looking into each other's eyes a light tangerine sunset behind them. And on the bottom was his signature and a statement that read: Sophie, the most beautiful girl I know. She looked up at him feeling terrible about what she said.

"I...thank you...why did you paint this?"

"I wanted to give you a gift. After you left I was thinking about you all of the time. And I wanted to express how I felt about you through this. I like you...Sophie." He said caressing her face. She closed her eyes leaning in to give him a kiss until his phone began to ring.

"Hold on." He pulled his phone out of his pocket and sighed once he saw who was calling.

"Oh is that your pregnant girlfriend calling?"

"She's not my girlfriend. And no it's not." Slyder defended himself against her accusations.

"That's not what she thinks."

"Sophie all I want is you. That's it. That's all I want." His cellphone began to ring again and Sophie rolled her eyes.

"Goodbye Slyder." She ran off into the drizzling rain hurrying her way back to her house.

She was relieved to finally get out of the storm and she ran into her bedroom slamming the door throwing herself on the bed. Thinking just how much Slyder had an effect on her. One touch. That's all it took for me to realize who He, was. One glance. Instant, burning attraction. One statement. "Is that too tight", he whispered in my ear. That's all Sophie wrote down in her notebook. Her hair, dripping wet with rain, handwriting in scribbles, Sophie tried writing something else. Her hand was shaky, trembling, she couldn't determine whether it was because of how angry she was, or how cold she was. Sophie searched desperately around her dark, cold, bedroom. She felt alone, lost and hopeless. She knew that no one, except Him, could free her from this remote trance. Her walls were covered with shadows from the trees blowing in the heavy wind. She was suffocating; the room was closing in and ruin inevitable. Mortification was the only freedom that she found fitting, pulling her toward the edge. Pathetic. Sophie could only blame herself. She was confused, but there's really nothing to be confused about. Inside, her mind, jumble of useless, heavy emotions and wounding thoughts, all of which were negative. Sophie punched her pillow and buried her face deep into its feathery abyss. She willingly transferred all her emotions and thoughts to her lifeless pillow. It was a welcoming, soft escape that soothed her deaden soul. Sophie's numb; heart and all. Her clothes were wet and heavy, flooded with tears and rain, and her skin pale and lifeless. She was shaking uncontrollably. She knew the rain would dry, but would her tears? At that moment, she didn't care, she couldn't feel, she just wanted to be alone with her misery. She wanted to spew out all of her frustration, her anger and her confusion. I just walked away. I can't believe I just left him there. Sophie screamed into her pillow as the tears started streaming down her pallid face yet again. Through a teardrop, her glance caught the crumpled, mucky, white canvas drawing lying beside her bed. It had been transformed into an abstract drawing of smudged pencil markings from the unforgiving rain. The torrent had made its own masterpiece of smeared nothingness that she didn't care to embrace. Her work tainted, she hastily tore the sordid abomination from its dwelling in her sketchbook and crumbled it with both hands before heaving it across the sullen room. She looked down at her hands still shaking and drenched with the sadness of her tears. She was unsure of what to do. The repugnant wad had found its way securely under her computer desk. Sanctuary, she thought, "even the rain's masterpiece of nothing could find safety in the shadows". She looked out the window at the unrelenting down pour. The shrill sounds of raindrops taunted her as they hit her bedroom window one after the other, begging the window pane to allow entrance into her perdition. The lightening flashed and the sky exploded into daylight giving the rain false hopes of triumph. The deafening crash of the thunder reprimanded the raindrops and she saw them roll down her window in defeat. Sophie found a little comfort in knowing that the storm was as angry as she was or maybe it's just making a plea, desperate for attention. Her phone vibrated with a text message that read: I'm Sorry.

'D'Artagnan's Theme'

Citizen Cope

The bell rang for the young children to go outside for recess. And they were happy to see that the construction on the playground was safe and complete for them to play on. Kids rushed to go on the slide and monkey bars. Others ran over to the teeter-totter laughing giggling and having fun. A little girl didn't know who to play with and decided to run over to the sandbox to build a sandcastle. A couple other kids joined her and they all began to build a sandcastle together. The little girl got out of the sandcastle skipping across the woodchips to the other side to get a better view. On her way over, her foot fell into the ground and some of the woodchips collapsed into a hole. She screamed trying to shake her foot free from what felt like a hand. It was caught on her stockings and the buckle of her shoe. She screamed even louder and the teacher rushed over to her aide helping her up from the ground. A mannequin arm surfaced from under the chips and all of the kids screamed and ran away. The teacher instructed everyone to go inside and stay there. She knelt down realizing this was the only section on the playground that looked like disturbed ground. She carefully lifted the arm and more woodchips fell and collapsed into a hole at first. But it was a domino effect and more and more woodchips gave way to a grave. The teacher backed away covering her nose from a rotten smell. She walked cautiously to look down into the grave and she screamed dropping the plastic hand down into the grave hitting more mannequin parts. A few minutes later cop cars pulled up along the curb hurrying over to the deep wide opening in the ground.

They called in for back up on the walkie-talkie and police radio. More police rushed over lining the opening with caution tape. Not far from there Ginger had been rushed into the hospital from excruciating contractions she felt that morning. The staff had been monitoring her dilation progress since midnight. She was breathing heavily with her mom holding her hand telling her it would be ok and to just breathe. She was exhausted, sweating, and in pain feeling like she was having an out of body experience. The nurses rushed in more blankets and towels packing them in on the edges of the bed and Ginger cried out in pain her veins and arteries outlined under her pale clammy skin.

More police officers came to the scene instructing on lookers to stay back. Crime scene analysts were down in the hole uncovering more and more mannequin parts seeing a few with blood splatters. They snapped photos of a friendship bracelet that was masked with blood and dirt. The nurses were getting Ginger prepared to push. All of the chaos and noise around her was giving her a headache and she felt faint. Her mother placed a cold washcloth on her perspiring forehead trying to reassure her. The nurses told her to spread her legs placing her feet flat against the bed telling her to get ready to push.

Crime scene analysts continued to uncover more and more mannequins until they began to uncover strands of blonde hair from under the soil. More cop cars showed up and fireman illuminating the whole corner attracting more attention with cops' still urging and instructing people to keep their distance. Ginger began to push and the pain increased immensely feeling like a sharp knife was shooting up inside of her. The nurses told her to push again and she did sweating breathing heavily the noises around her sounding like a blur. There was panic and chaos all around the corner and surrounding neighborhoods. The analysts kept digging and saw a human forehead emerging from the ground. Ginger kept pushing and the nurses began to see the head of the baby. They told her to continue and just a few more pushes. They kept uncovering more and more parts of a human. They began to see dirty blonde hair and uncovered the face of a young girl. The nurses saw the face of the baby encouraging Ginger to keep going and they were easing it out.

They eased it out from under the dirt exposing a girl dirt and bugs on parts of her face and her arms sprawled out like she was on a cross finally free from darkness. Her eyes fell open. The nurses pulled out the rest of the baby, and they all realized that it was still.

CPSIA information can be obtained
at www.ICGtesting.com
Printed in the USA
LVHW040853300720
661936LV00002B/263